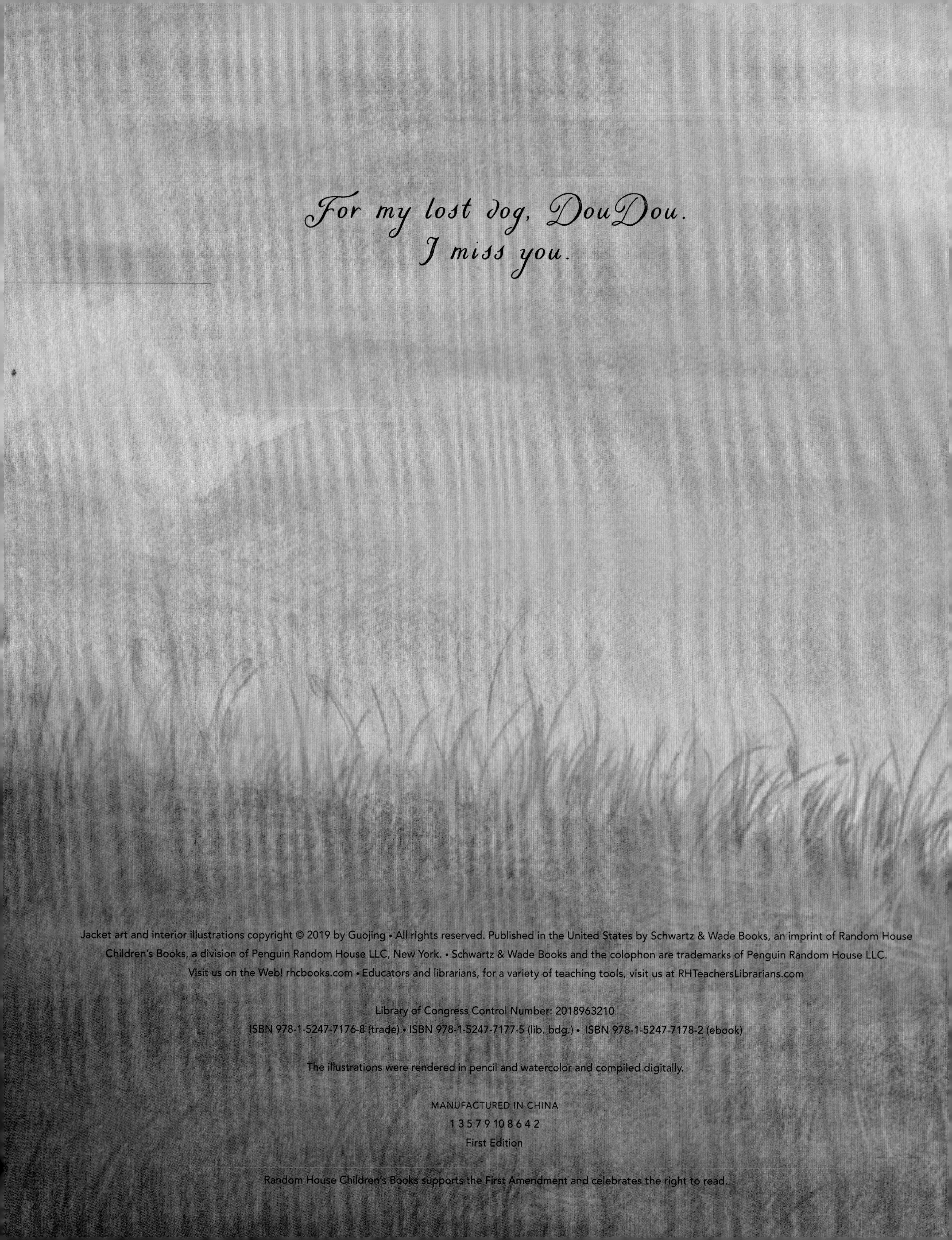

For my lost dog, DouDou.
I miss you.

 Published in the United States by Schwartz & Wade Books, an imprint of Random House Children's Books, a division of Penguin Random House LLC, New York. • Schwartz & Wade Books and the colophon are trademarks of Penguin Random House LLC.
Visit us on the Web! rhcbooks.com • Educators and librarians, for a variety of teaching tools, visit us at RHTeachersLibrarians.com

Library of Congress Control Number: 2018963210
ISBN 978-1-5247-7176-8 (trade) • ISBN 978-1-5247-7177-5 (lib. bdg.) • ISBN 978-1-5247-7178-2 (ebook)

The illustrations were rendered in pencil and watercolor and compiled digitally.

MANUFACTURED IN CHINA
1 3 5 7 9 10 8 6 4 2
First Edition

Stormy

a story about
finding
a forever
home

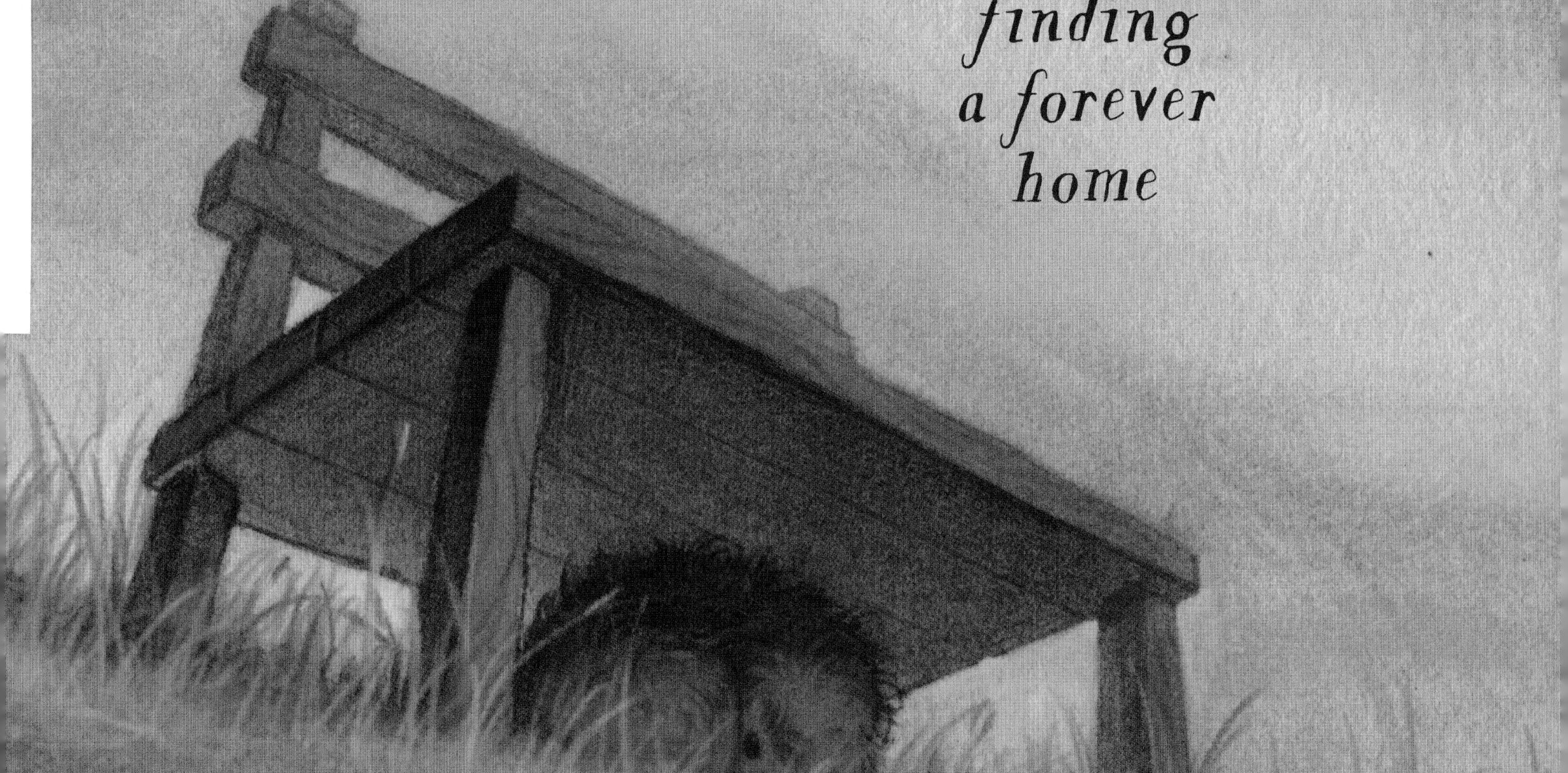

by GUOJING

schwartz & wade books · new york

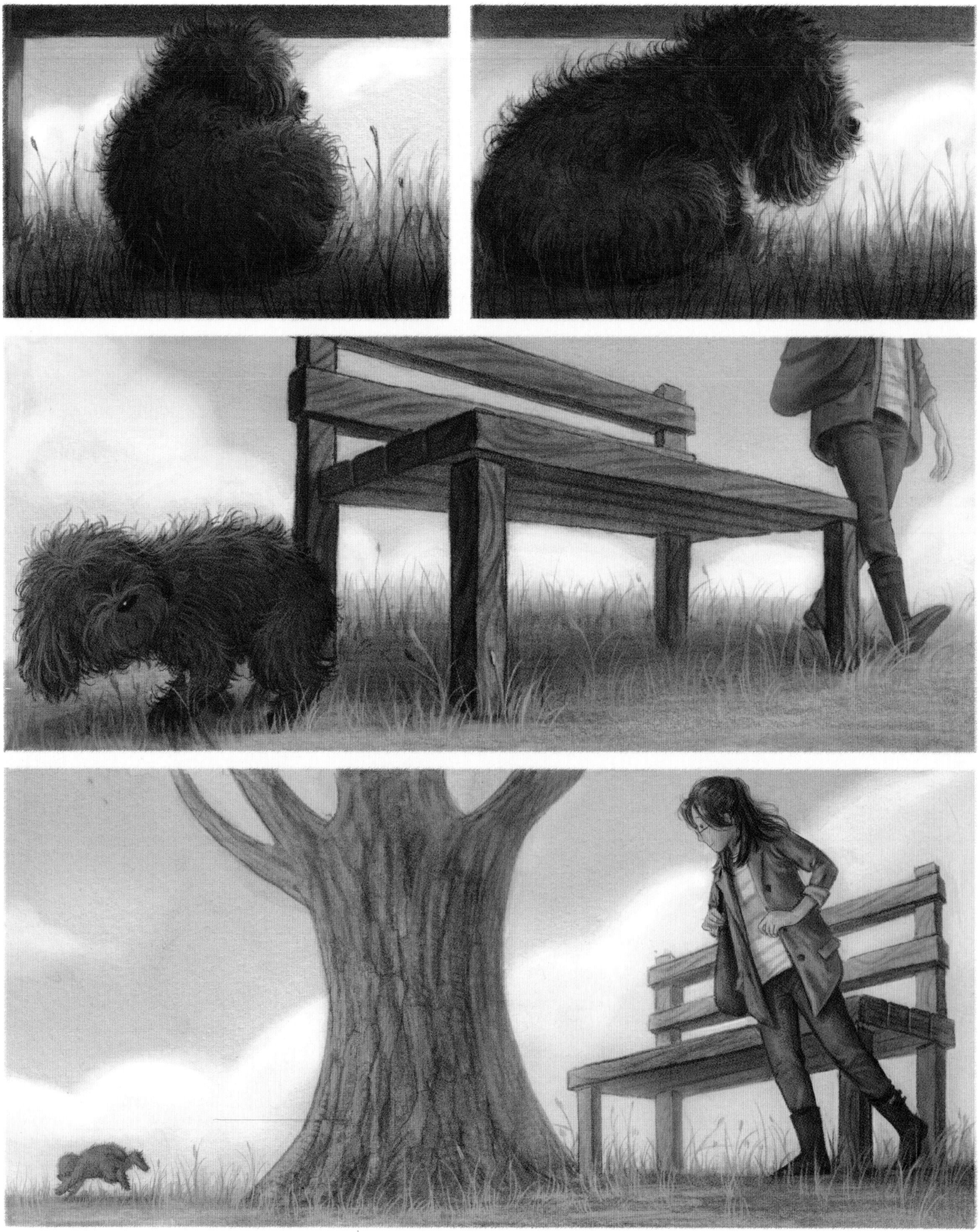

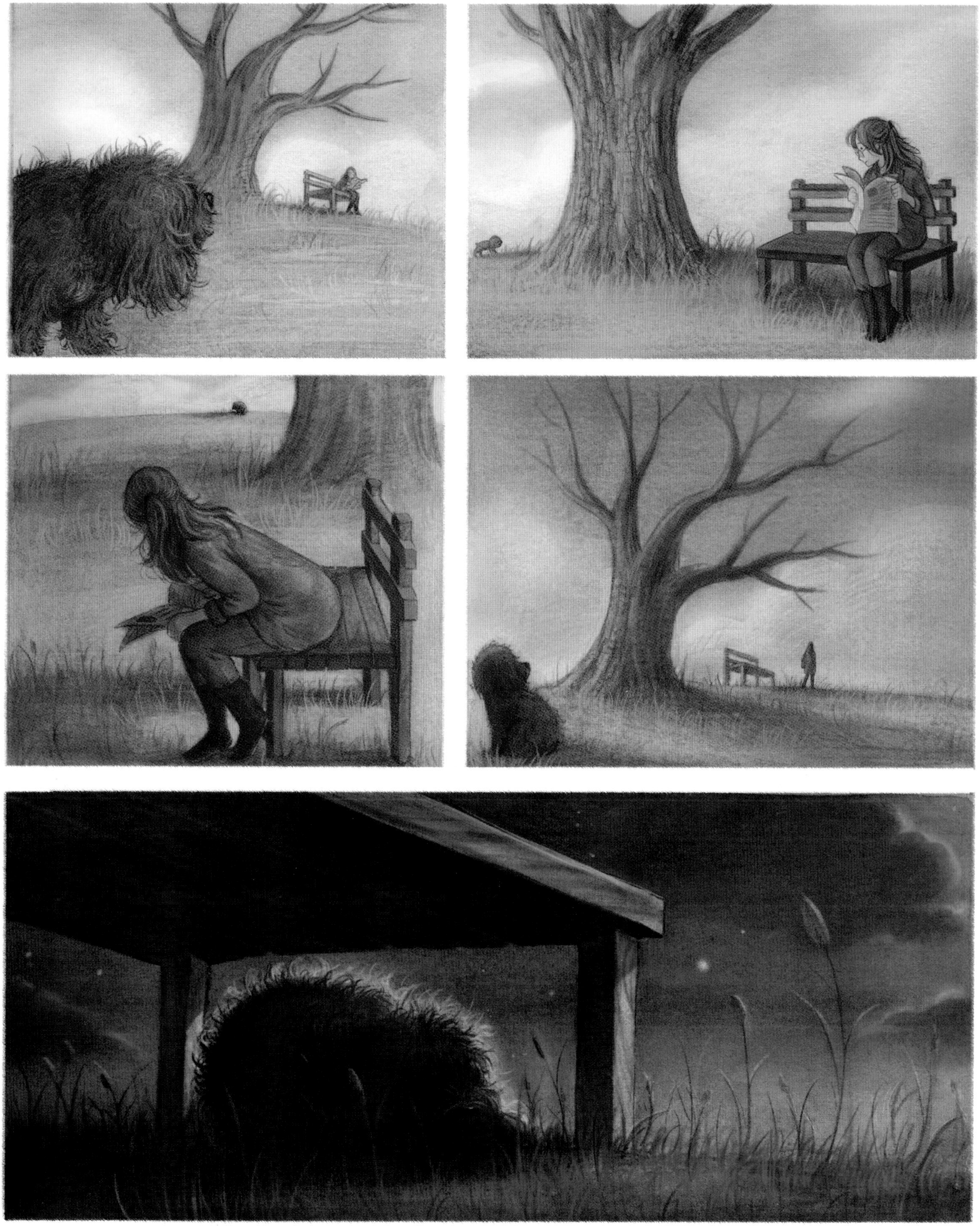

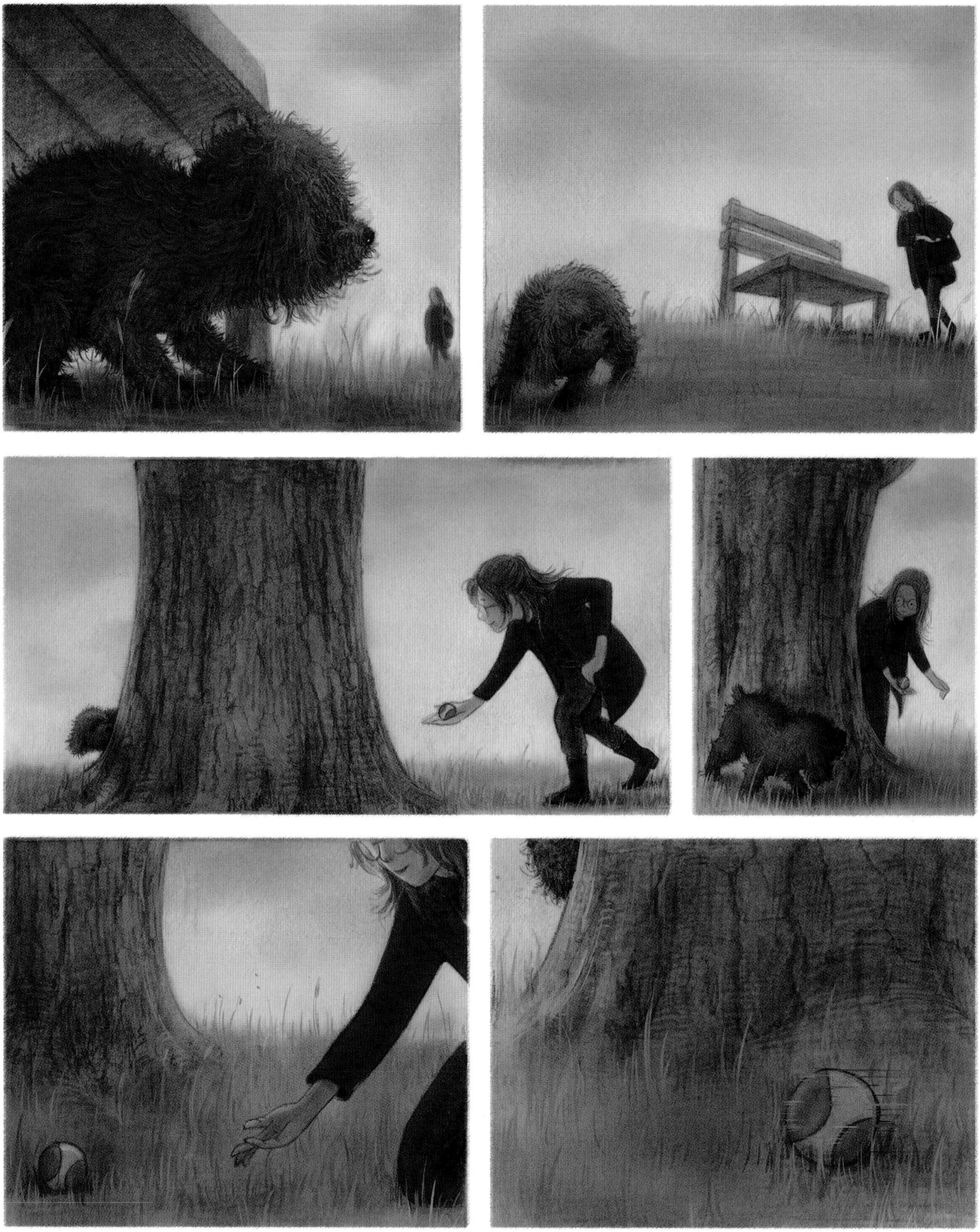

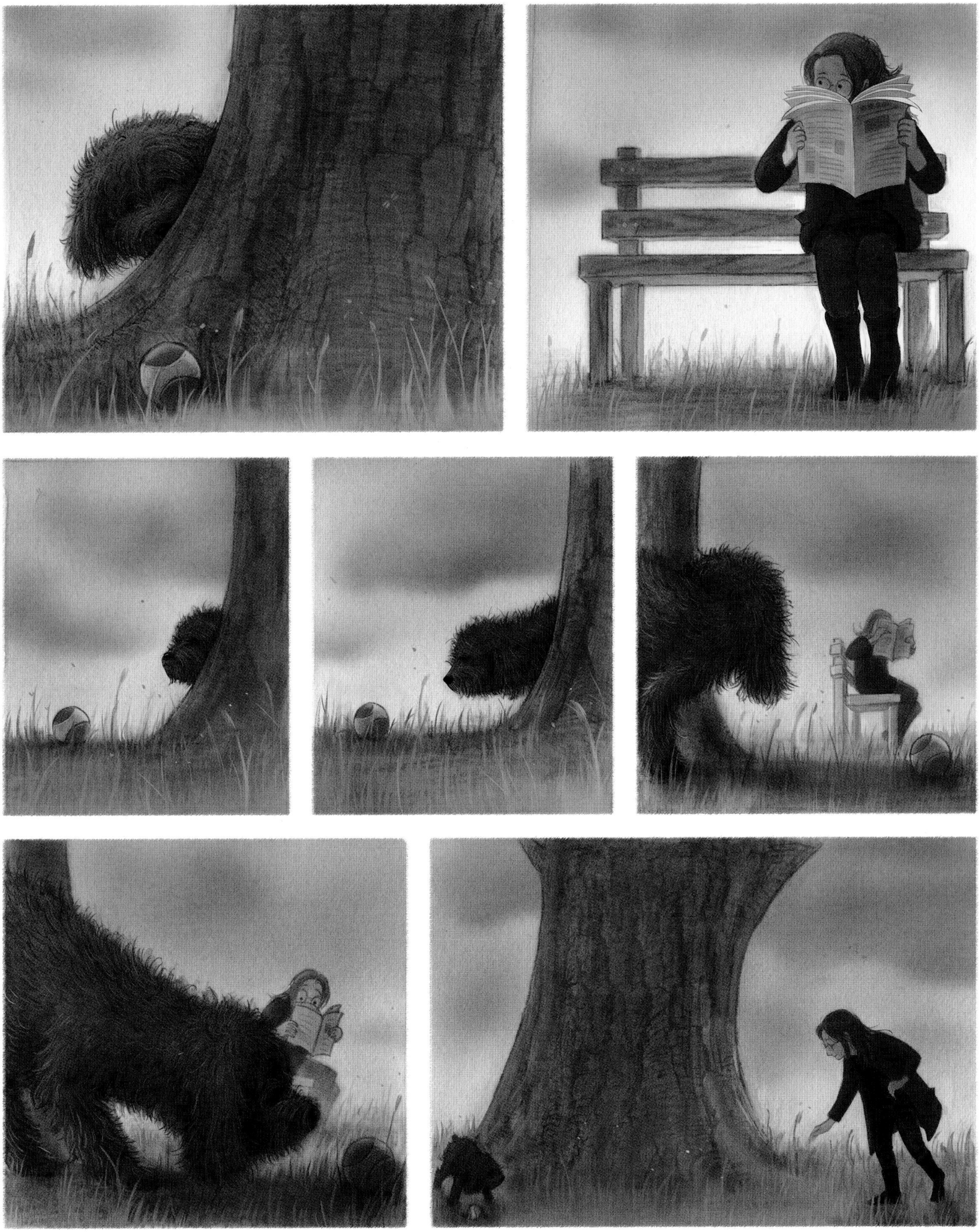

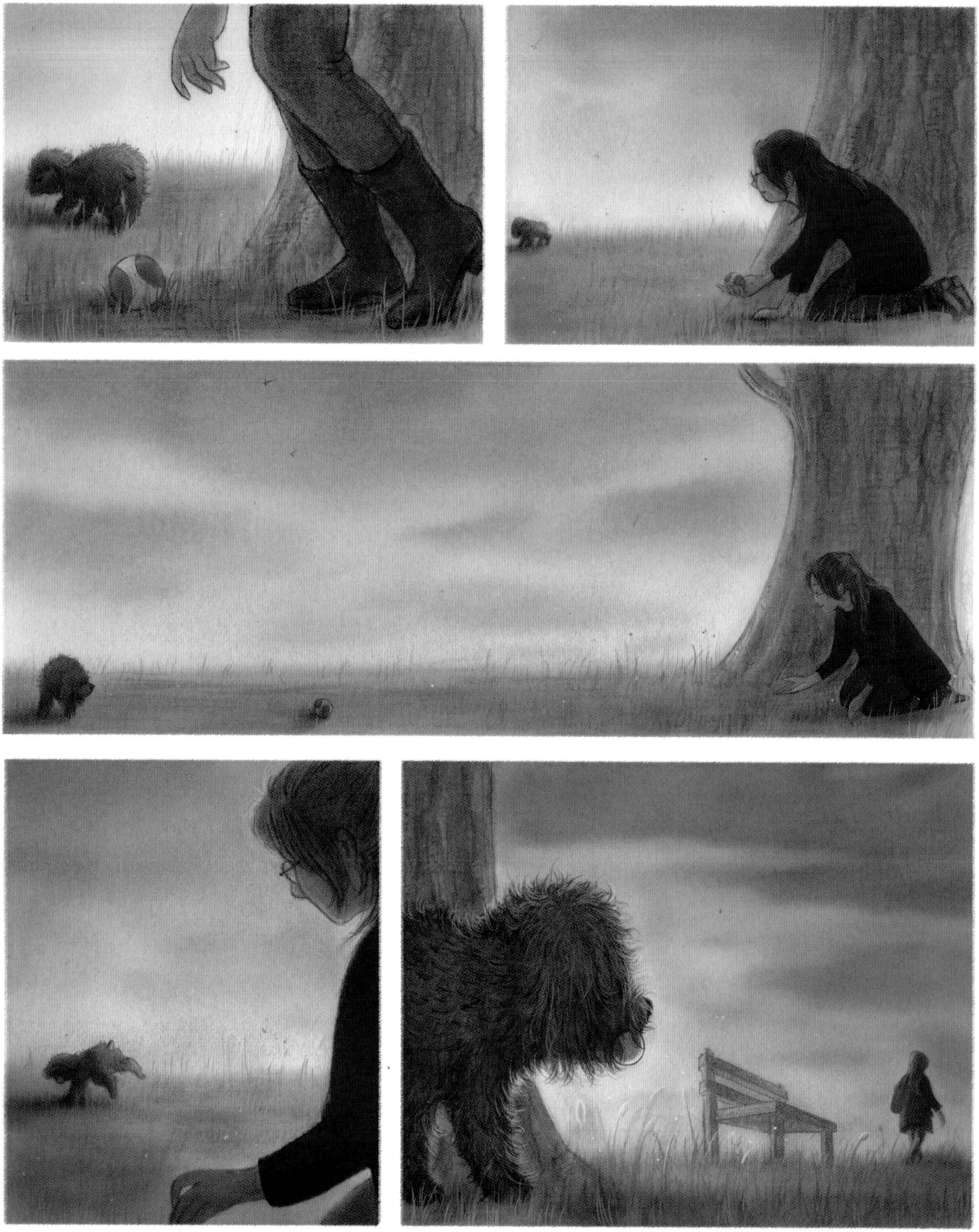

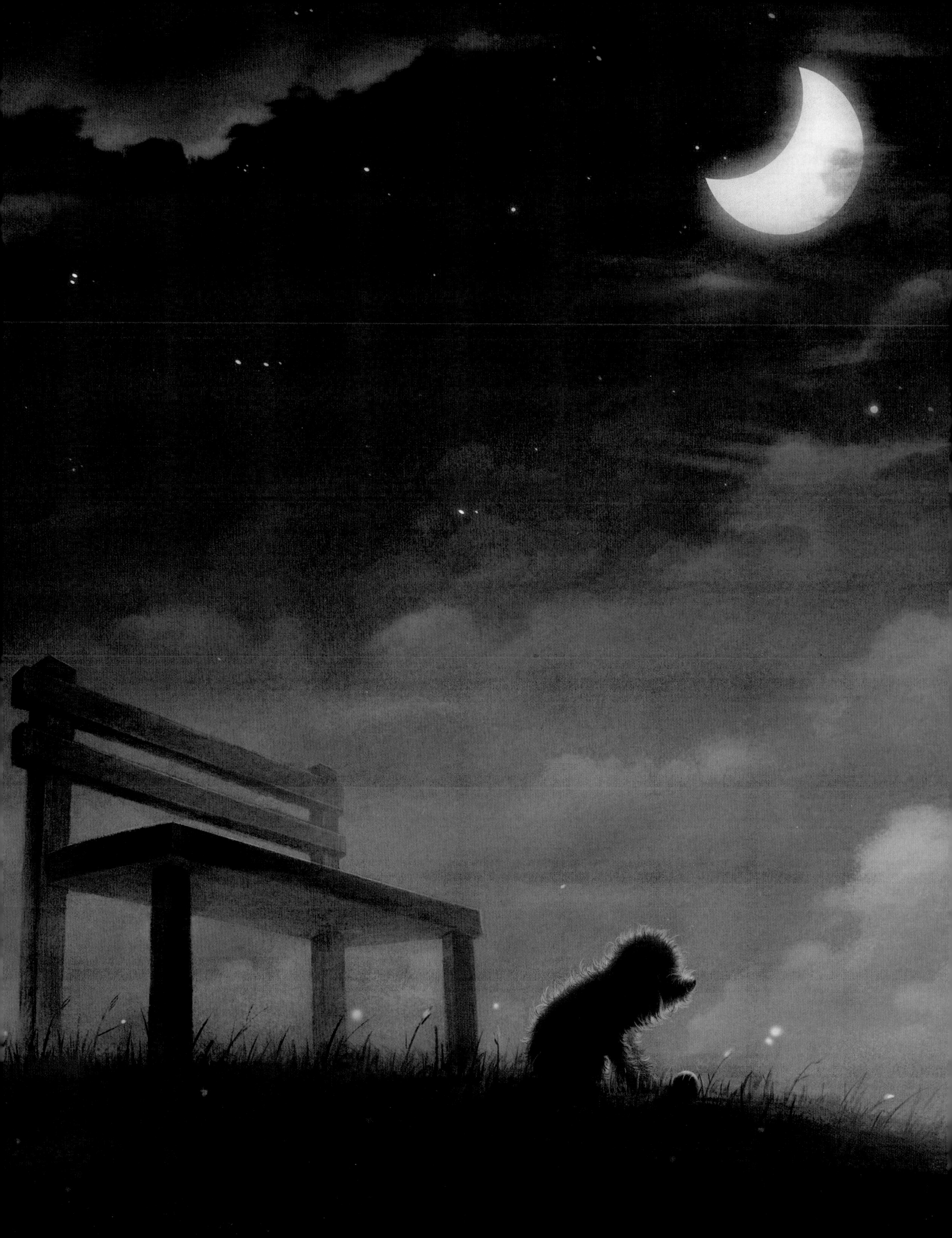

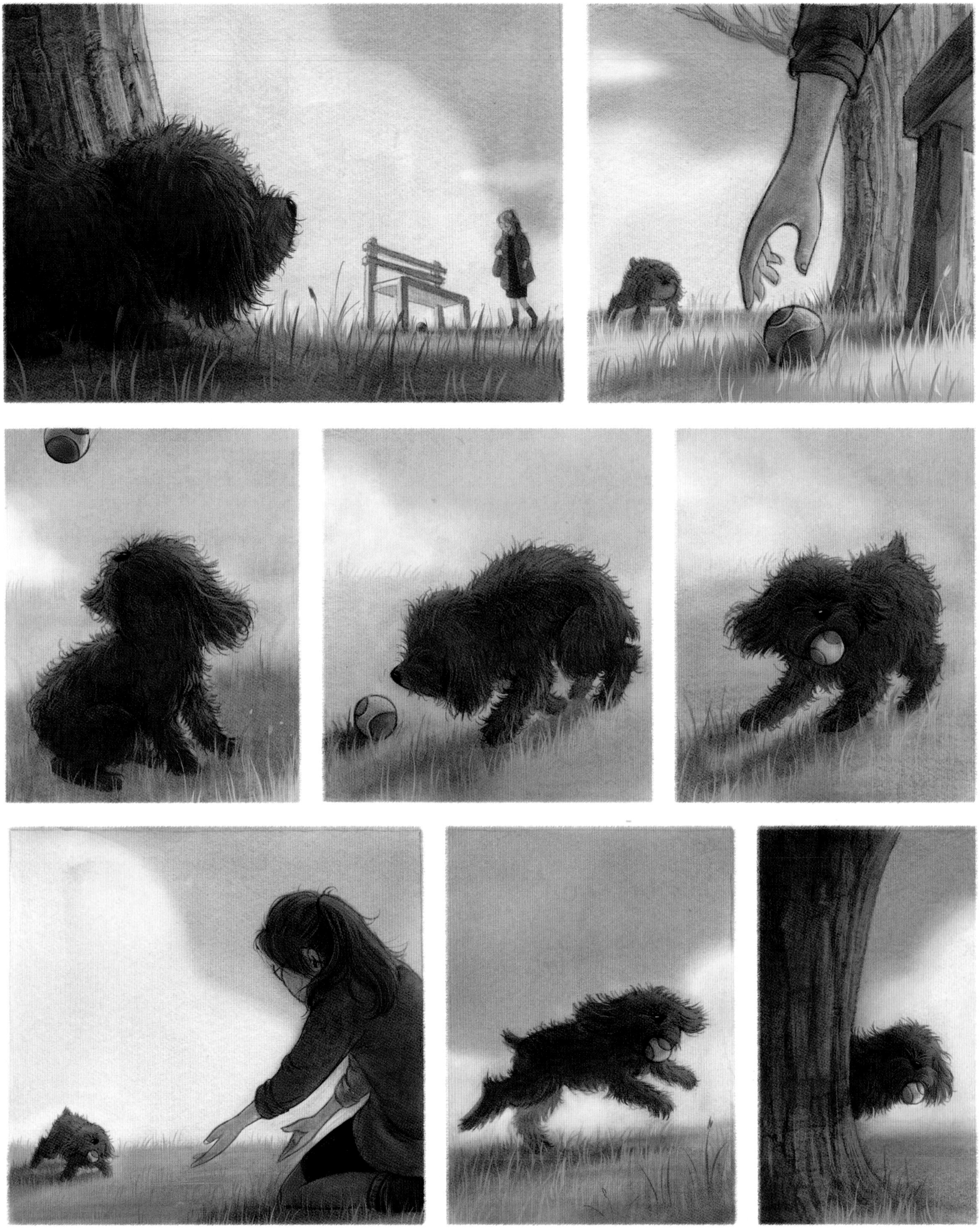

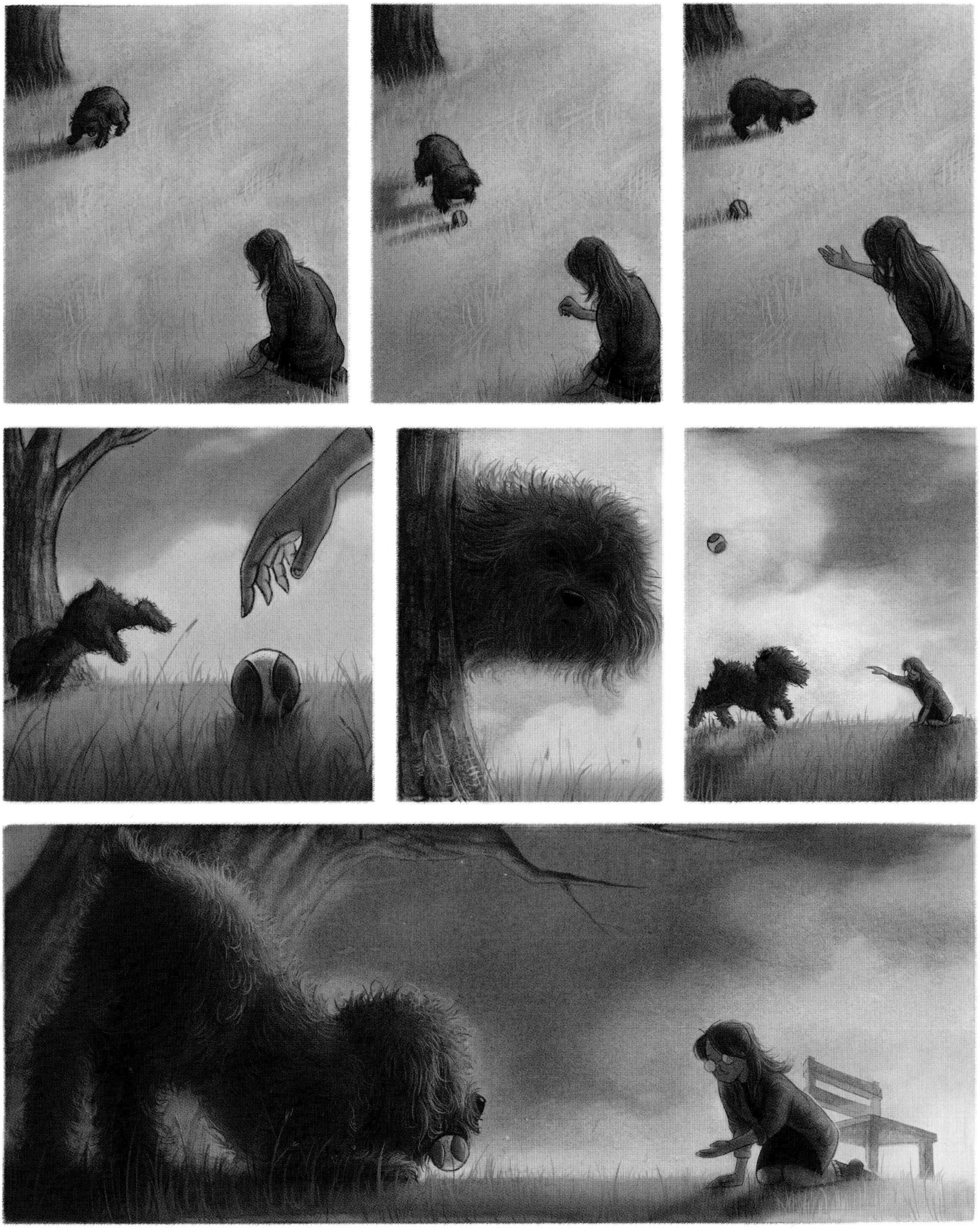

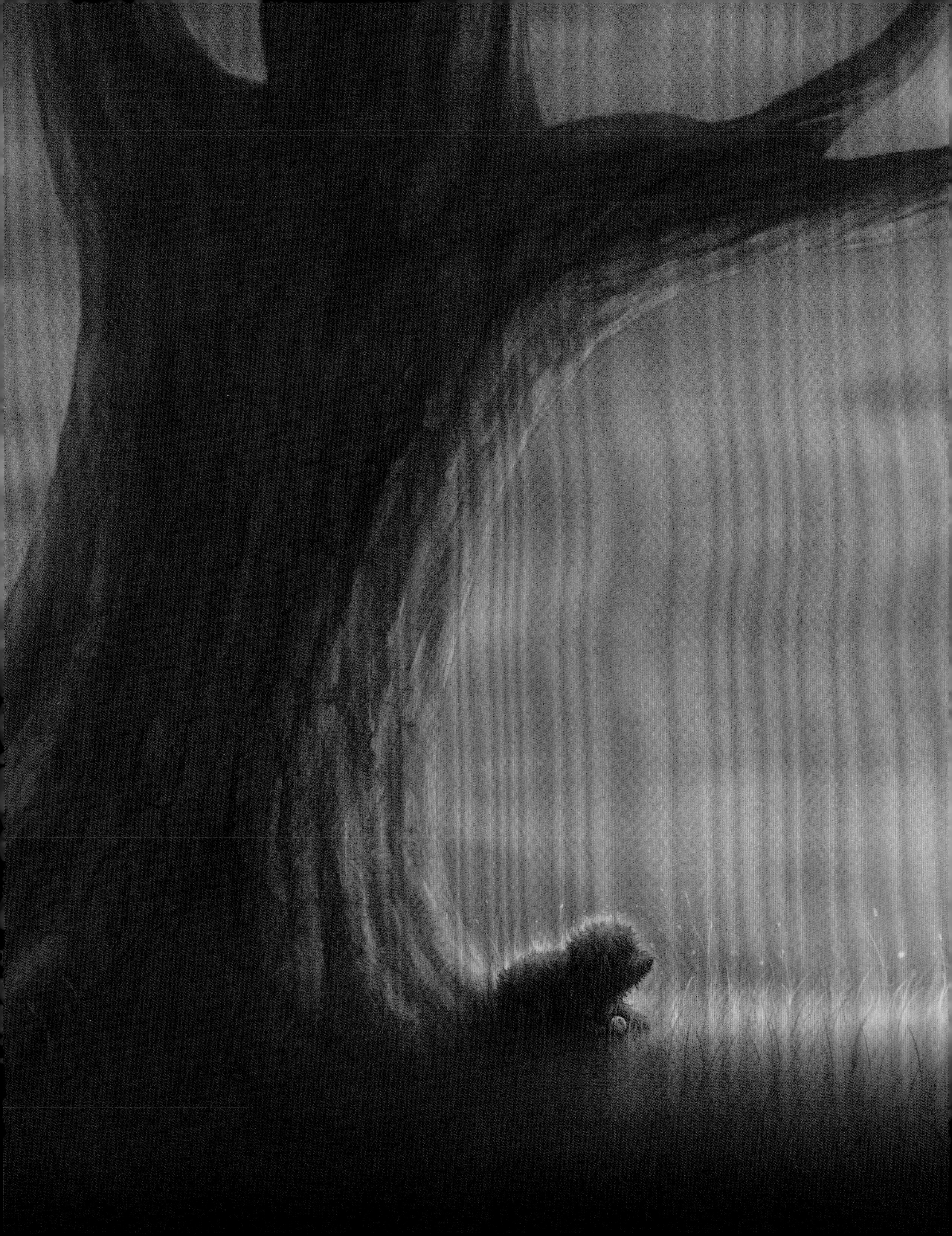

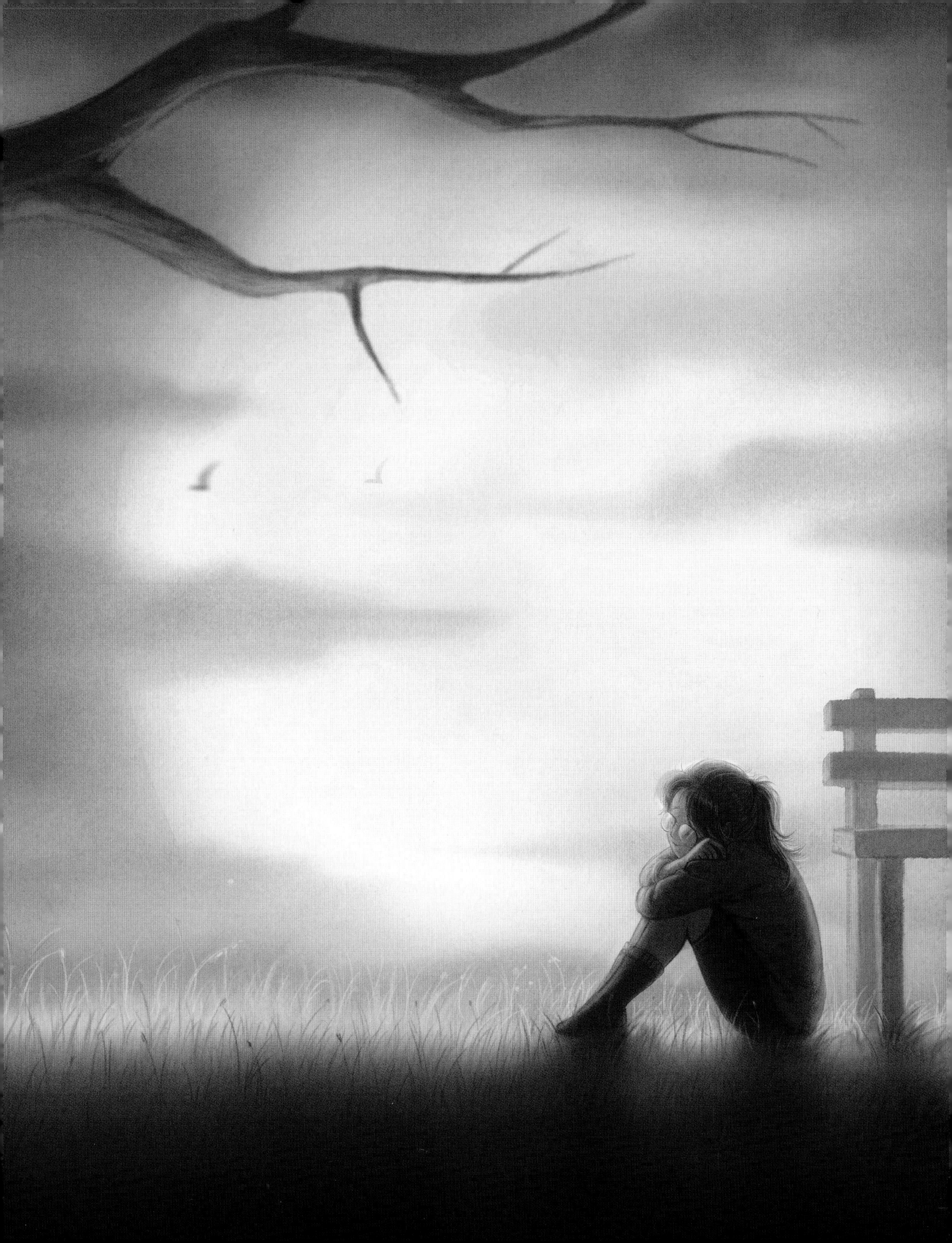

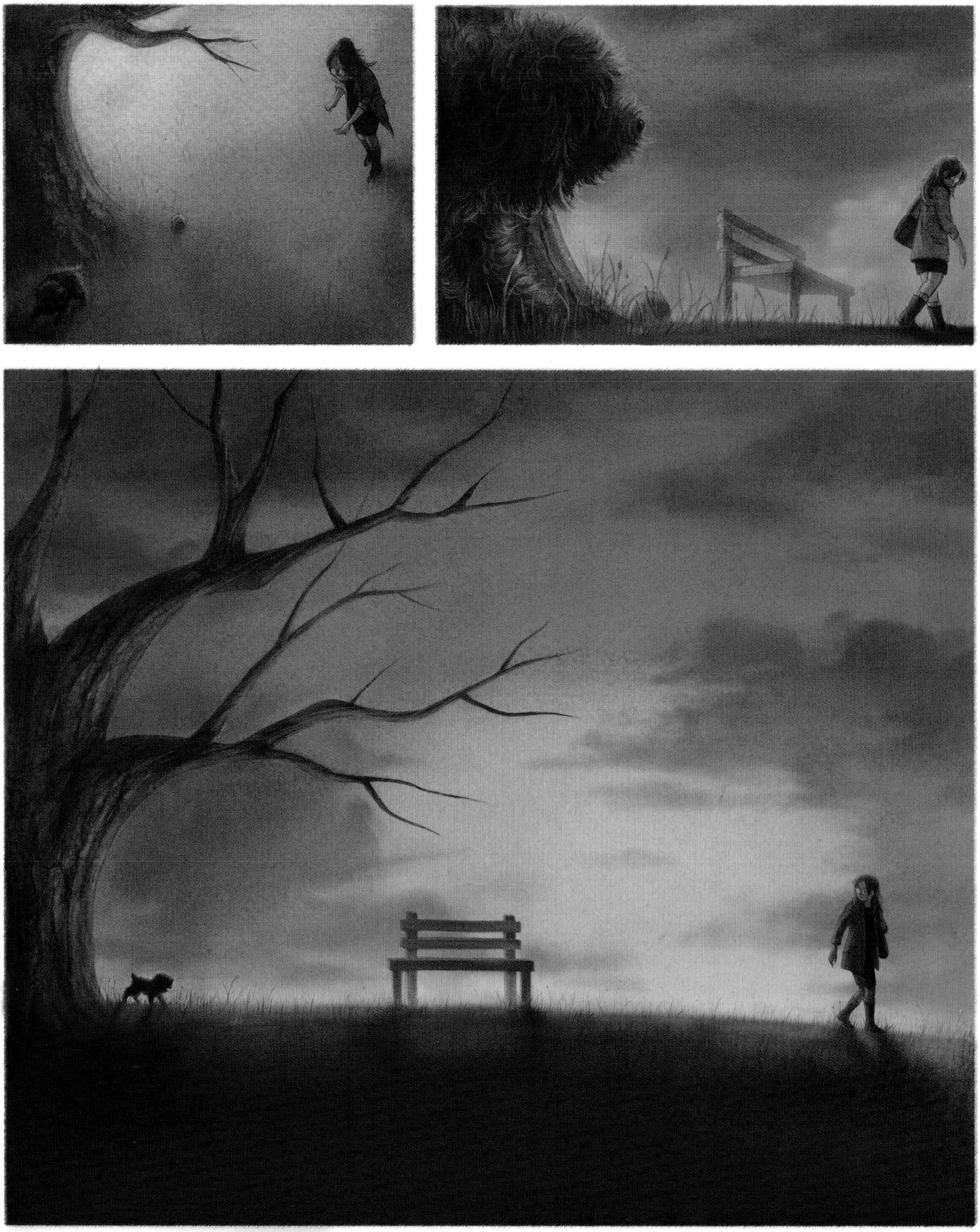

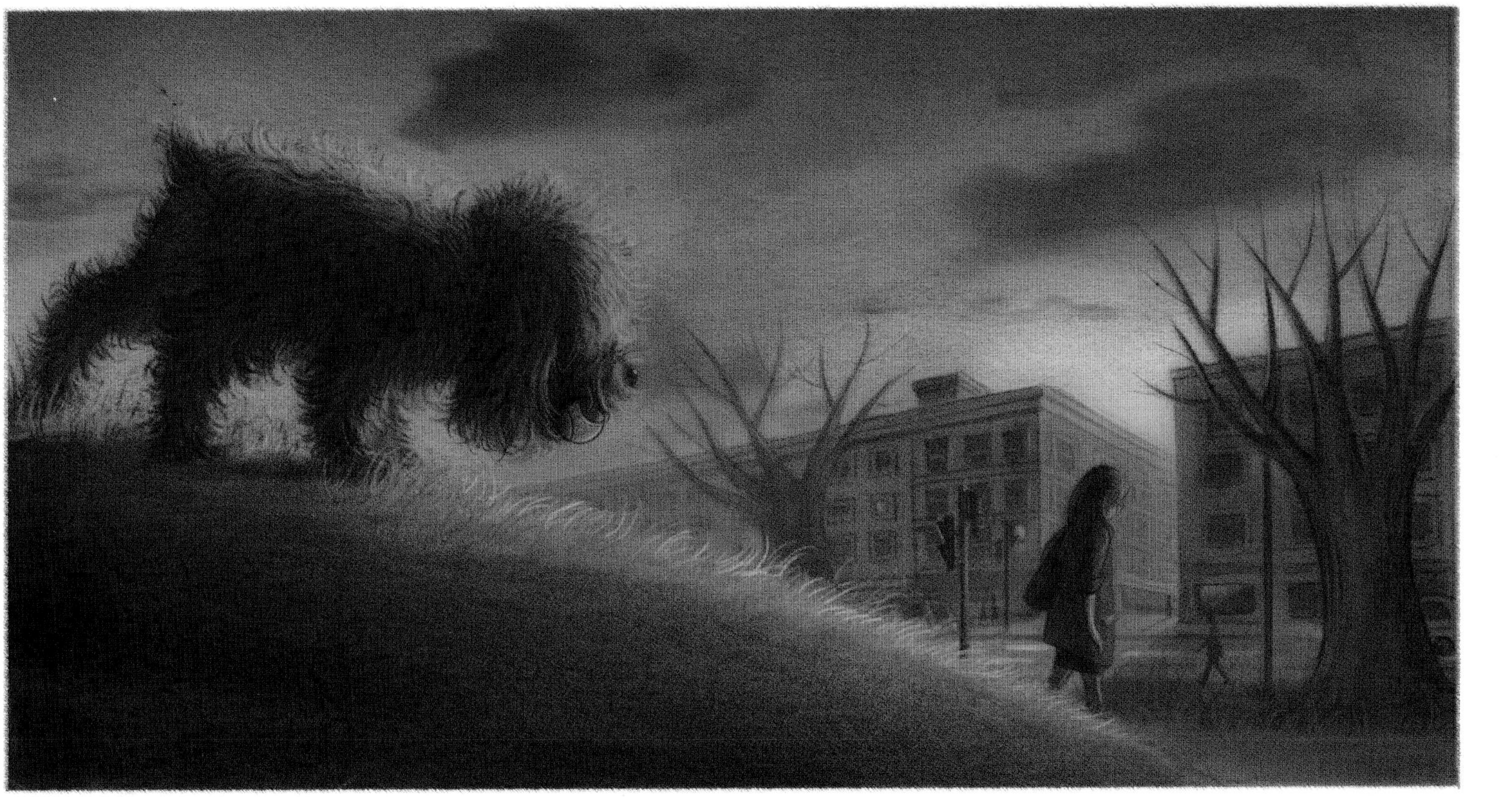

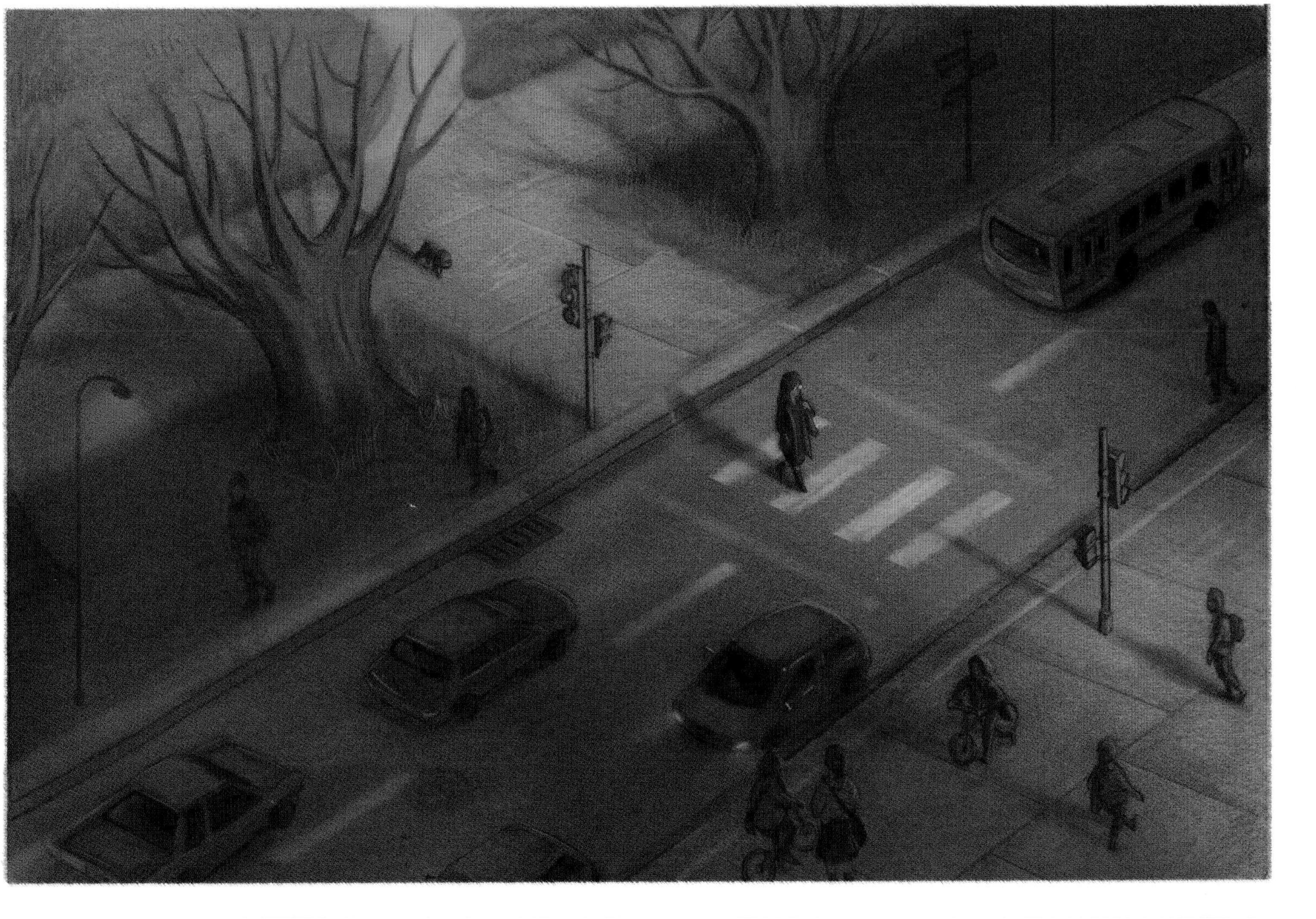

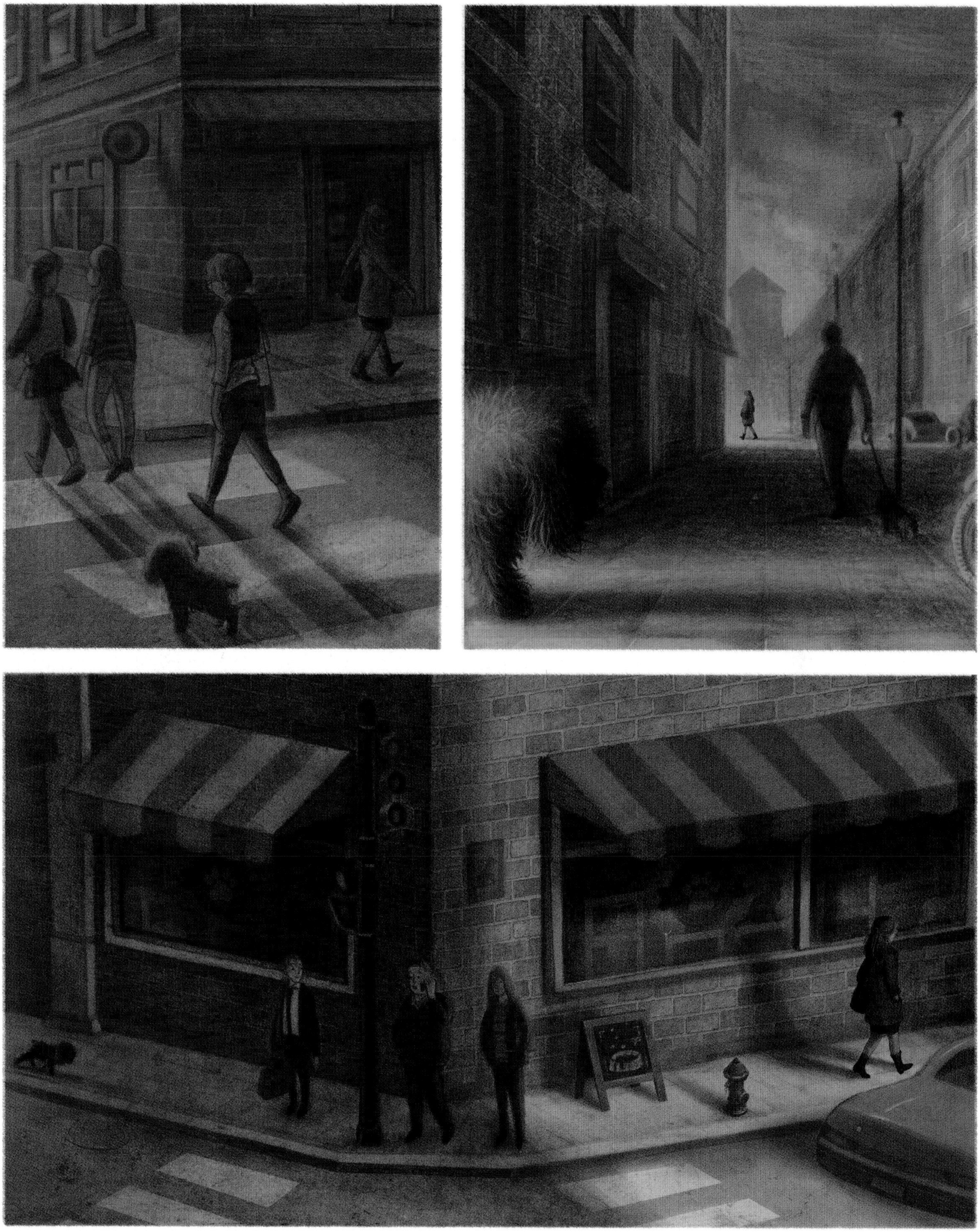

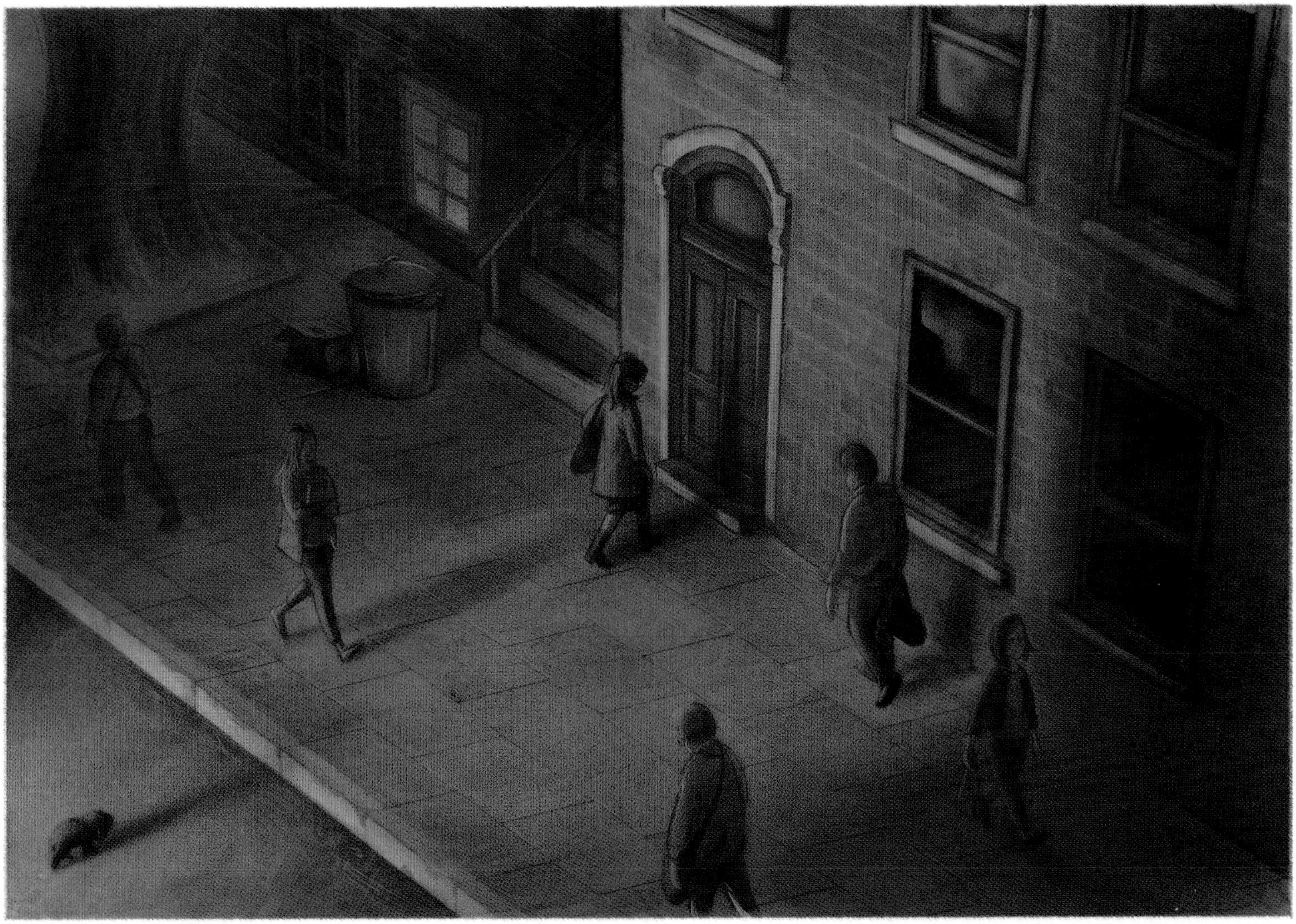
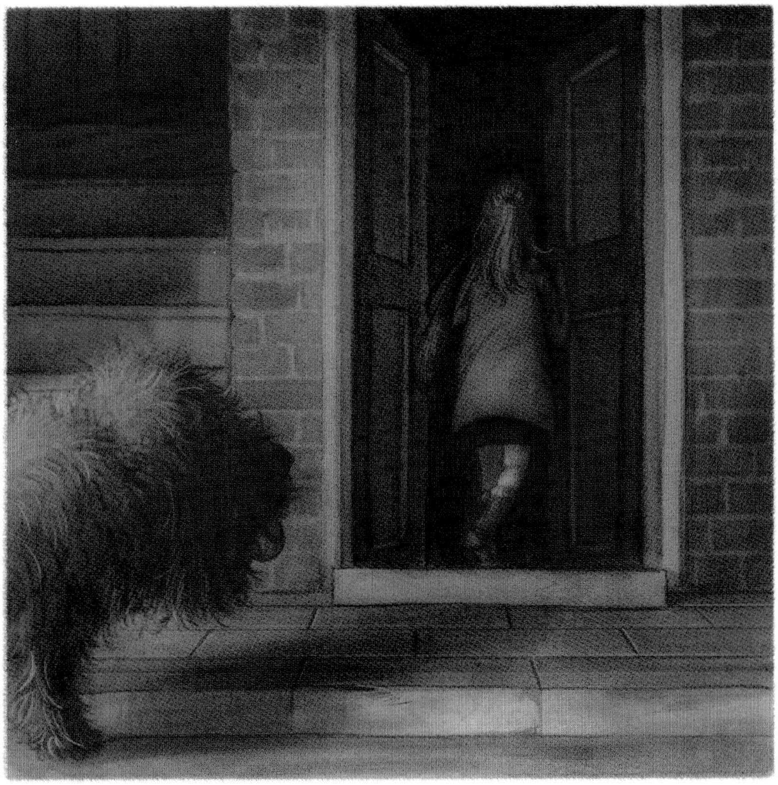
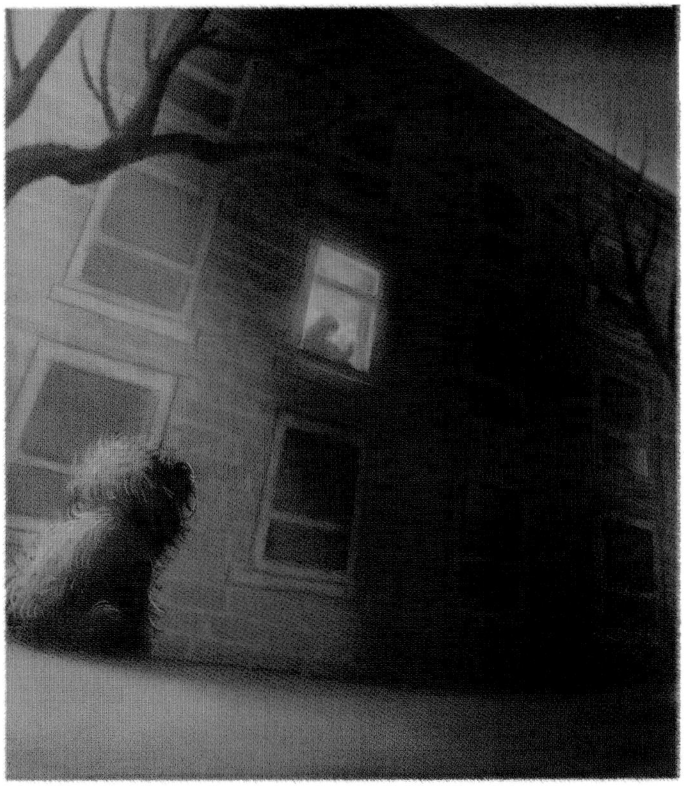

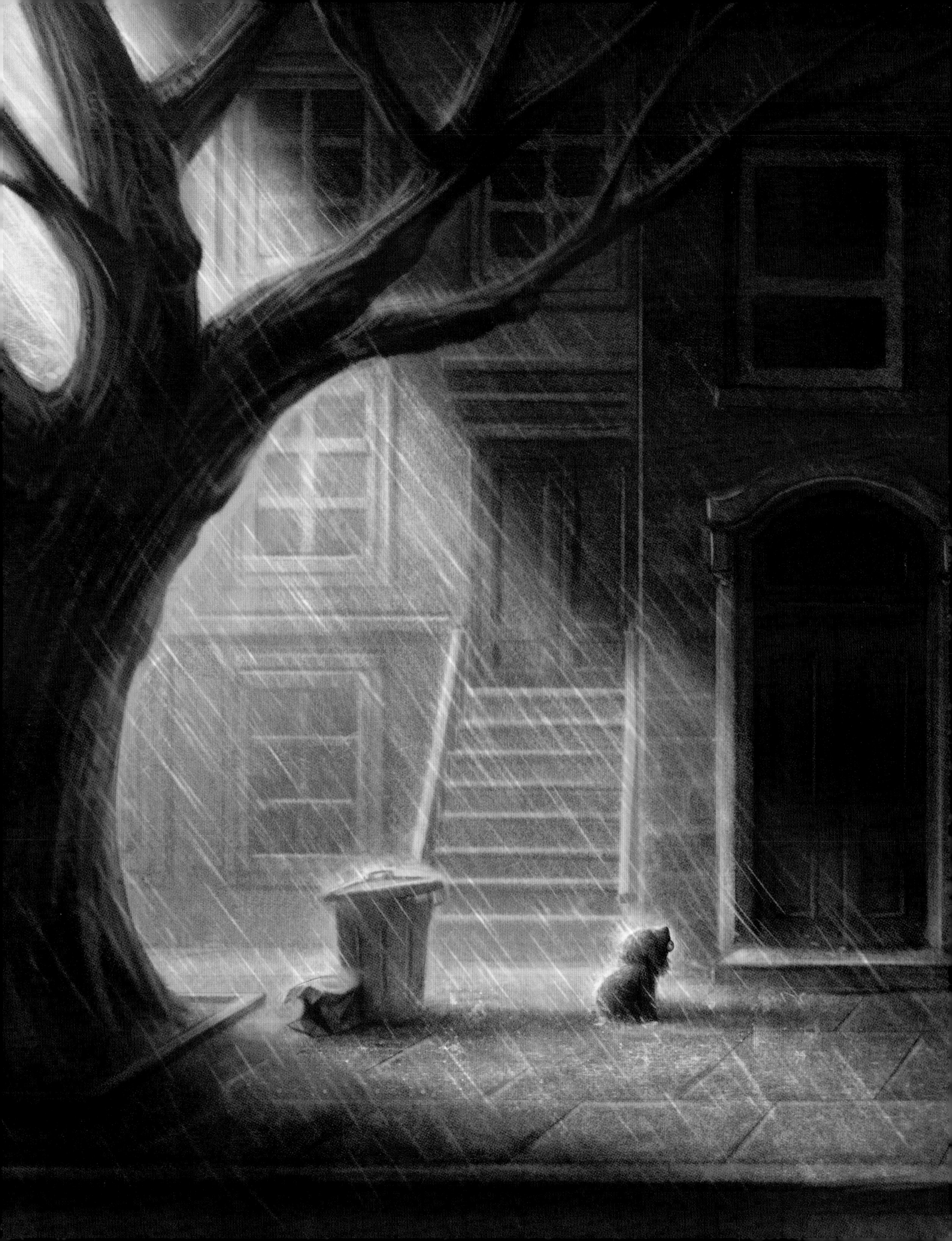

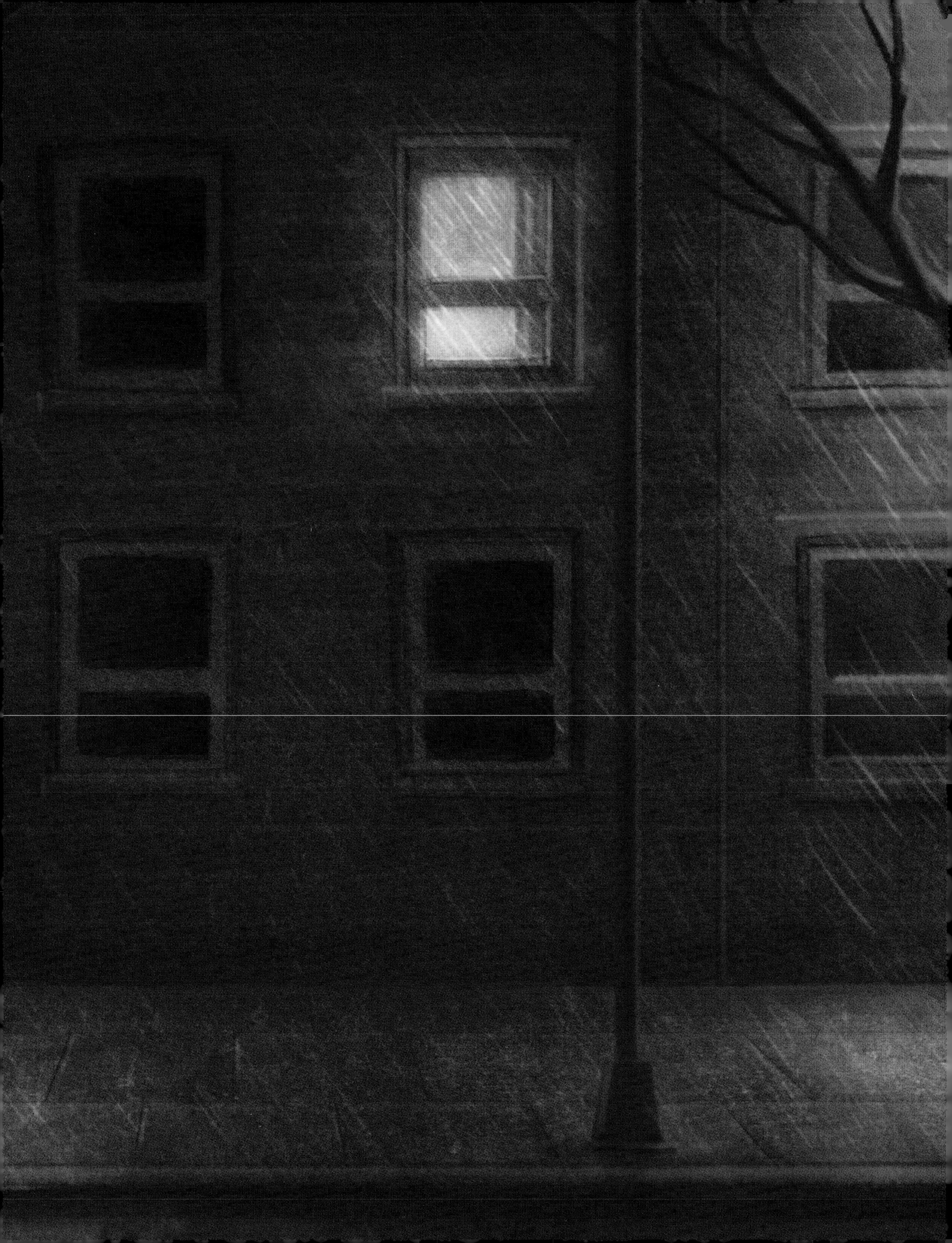

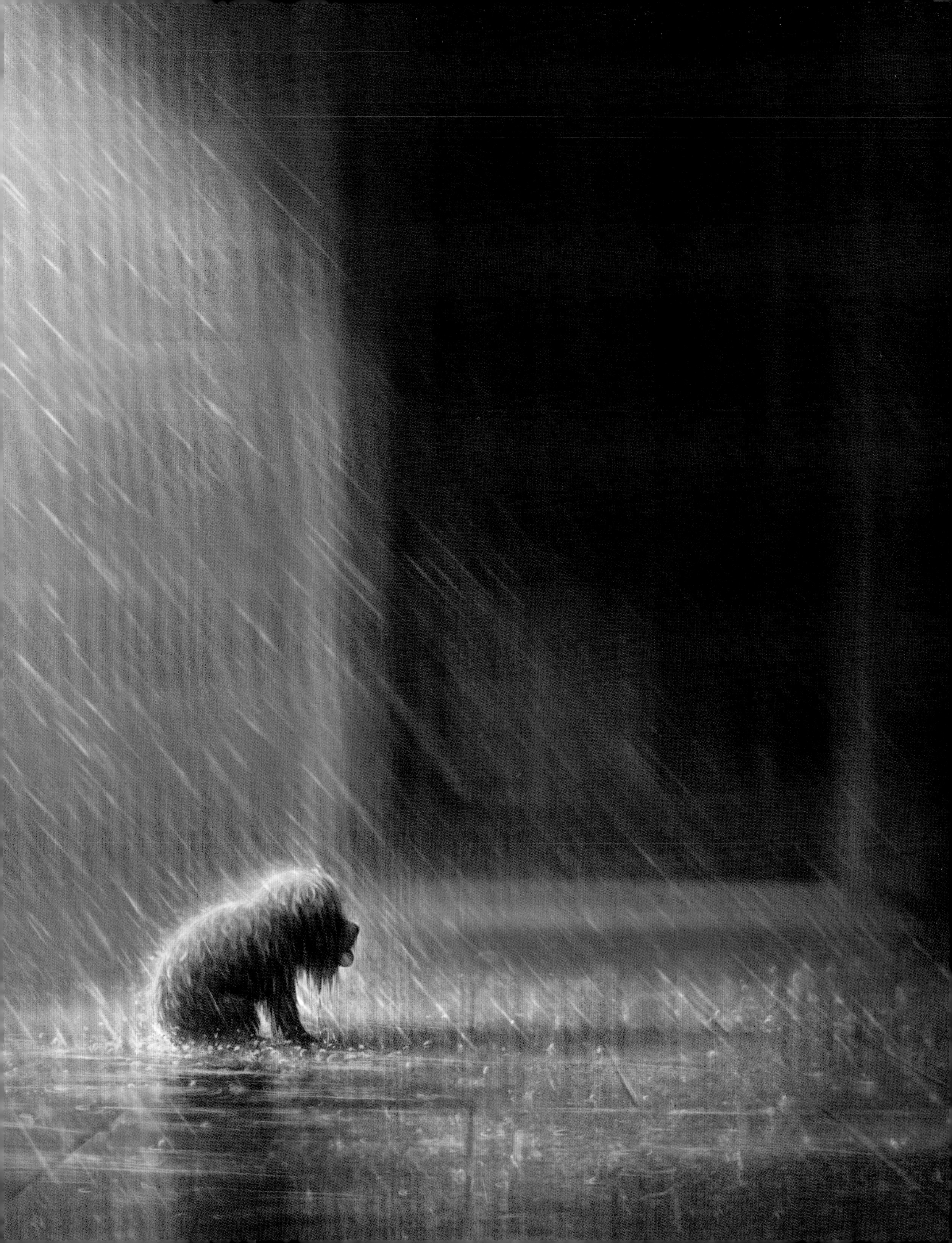

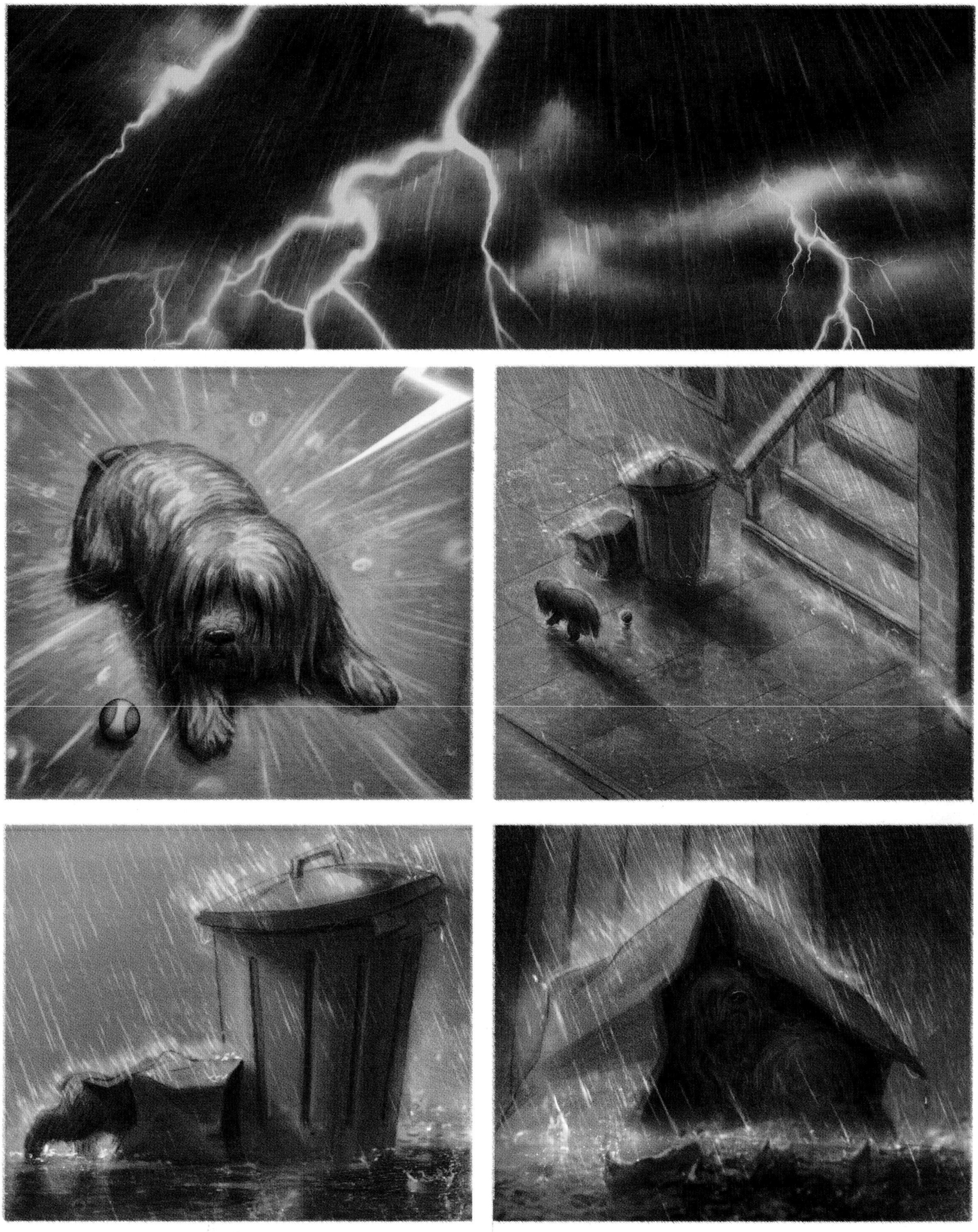

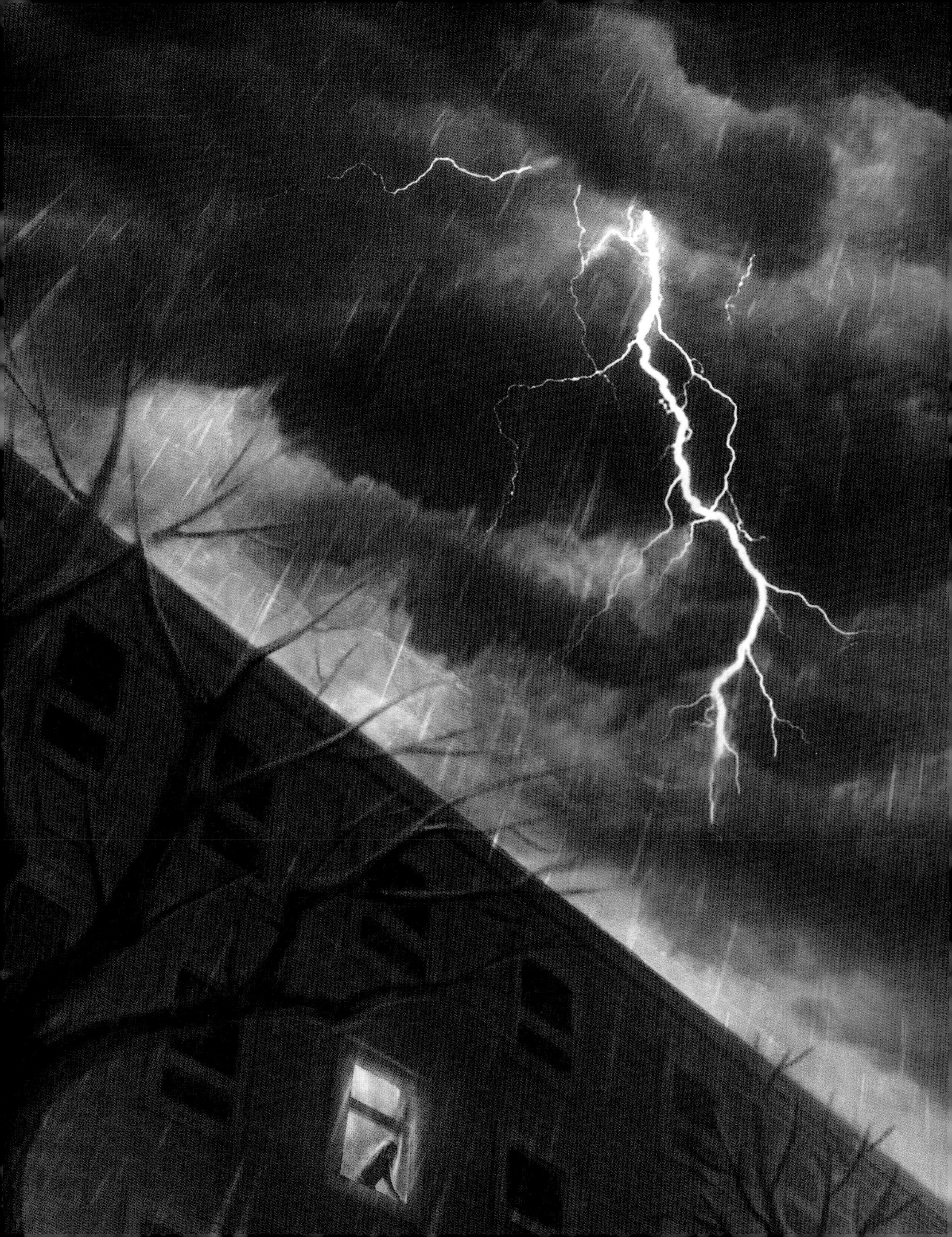

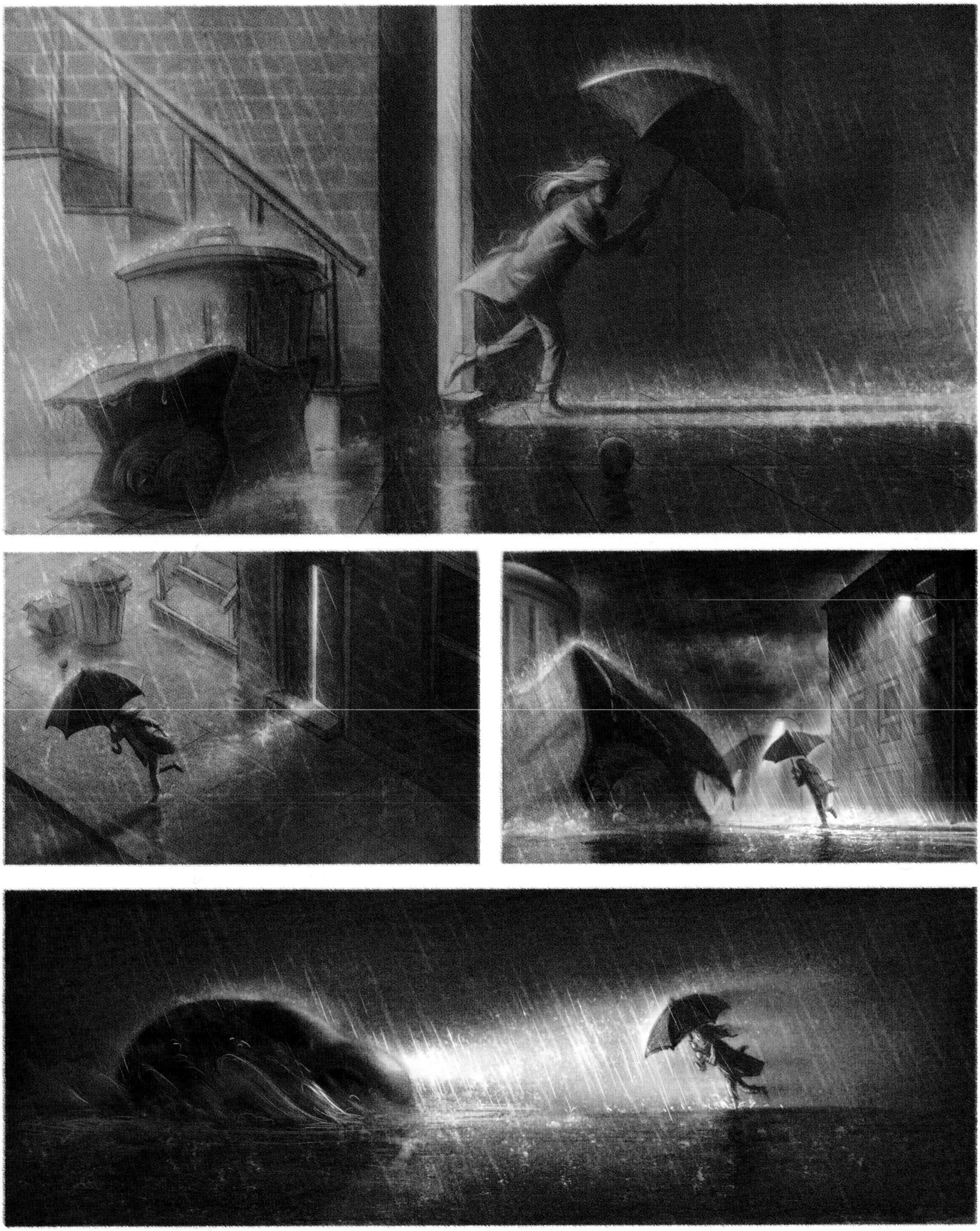

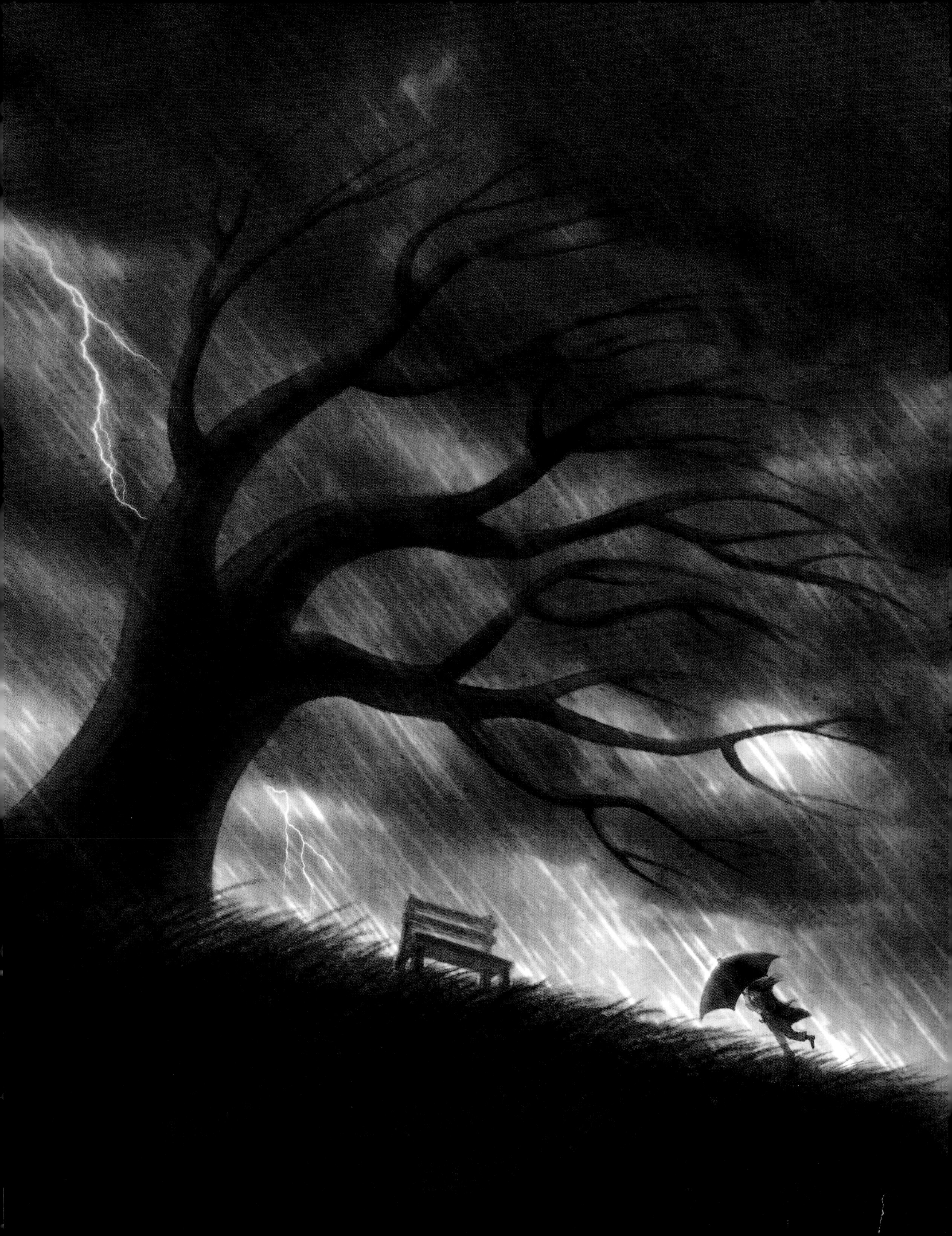

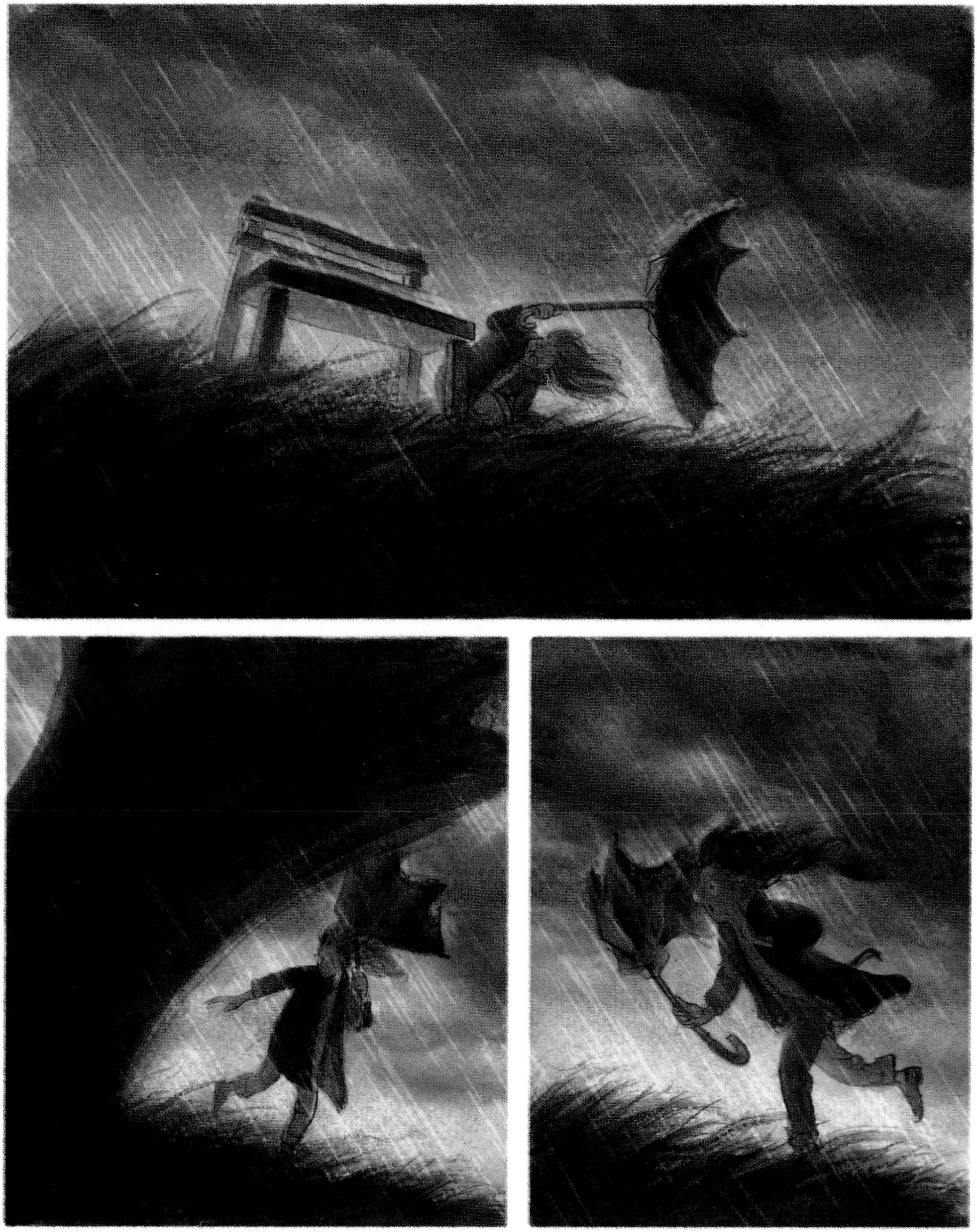

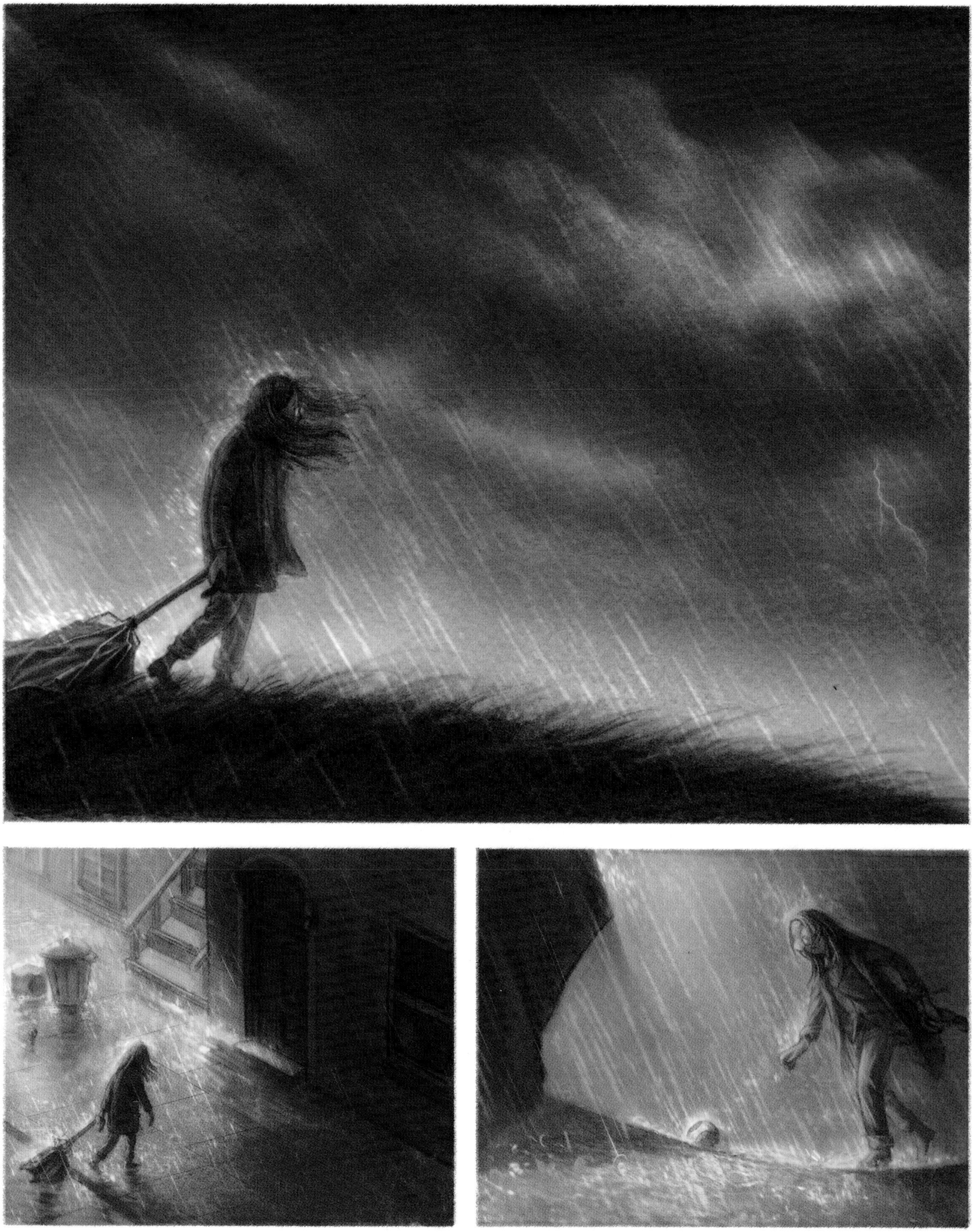

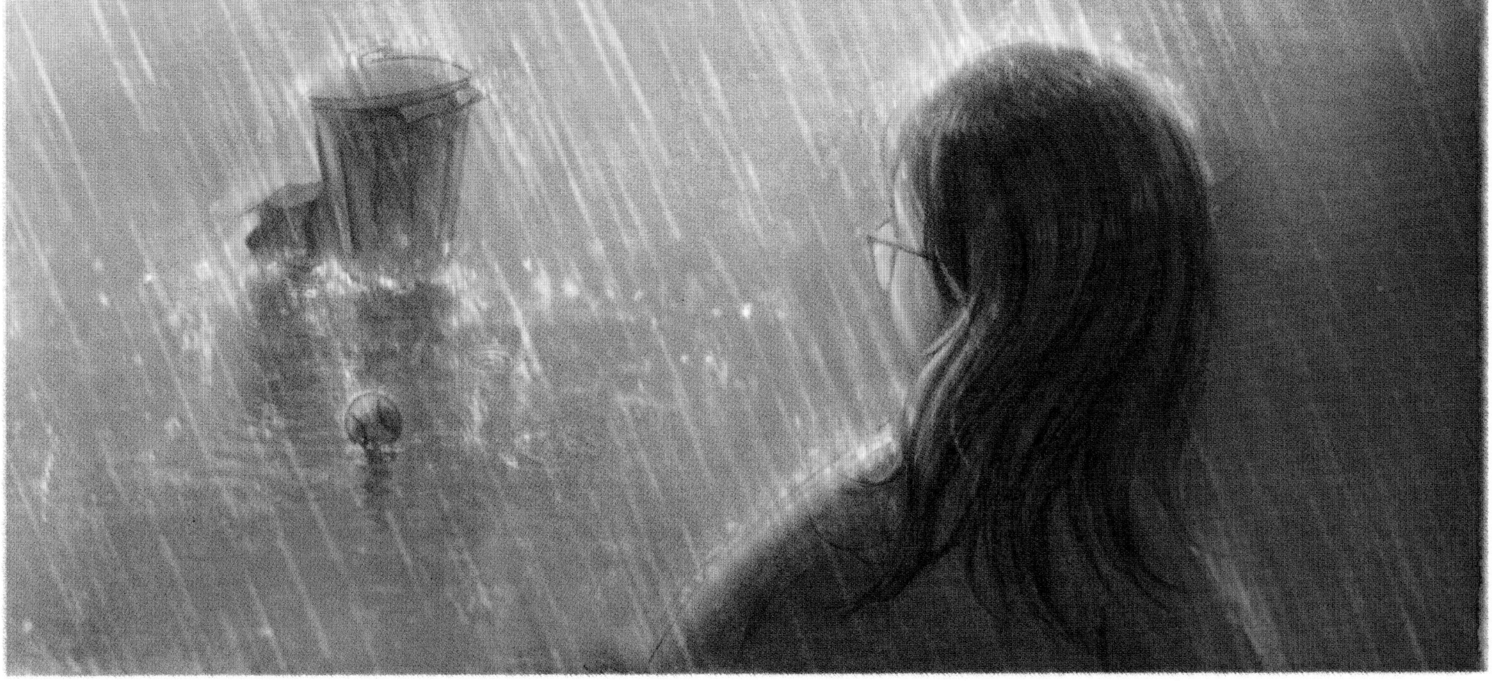
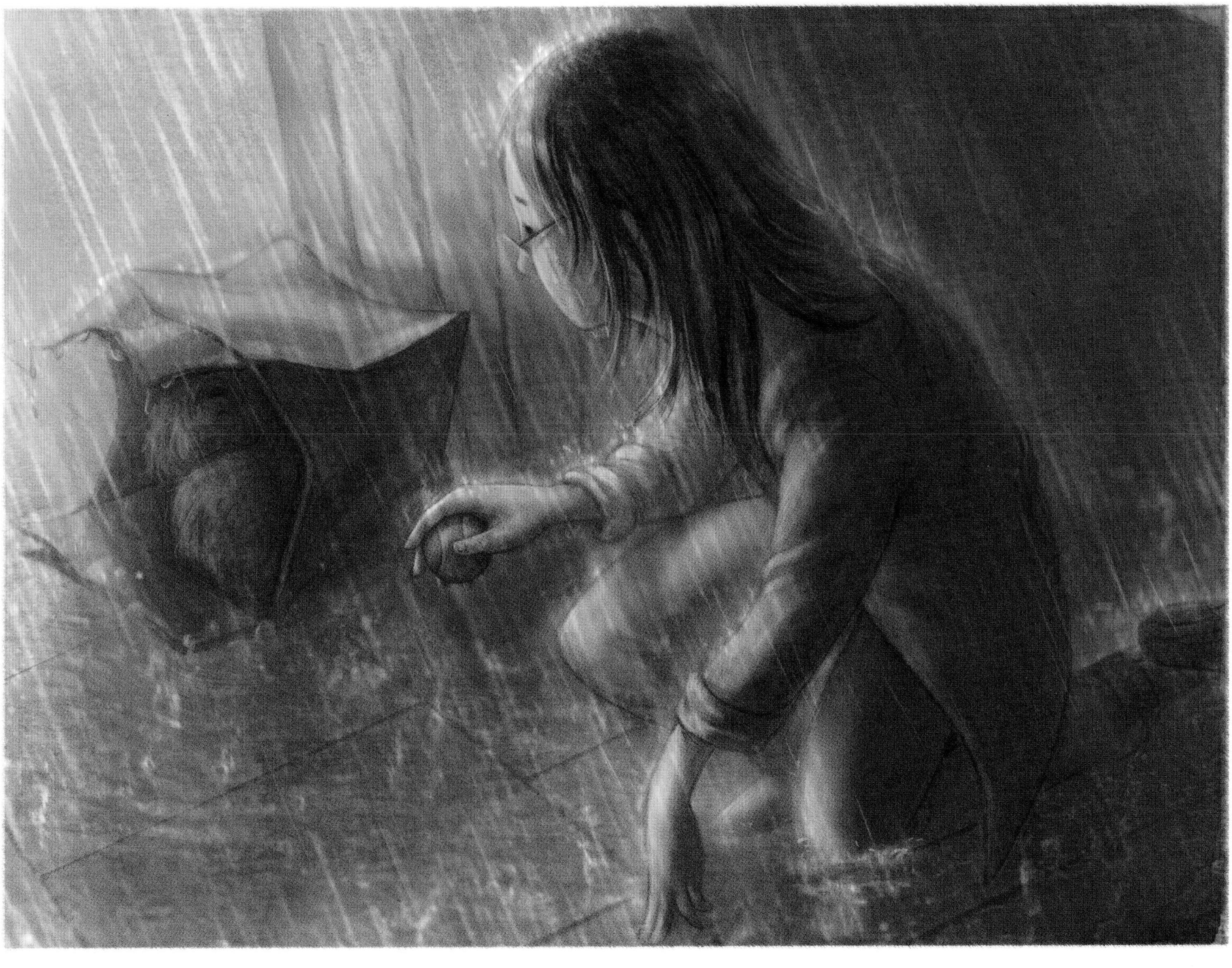

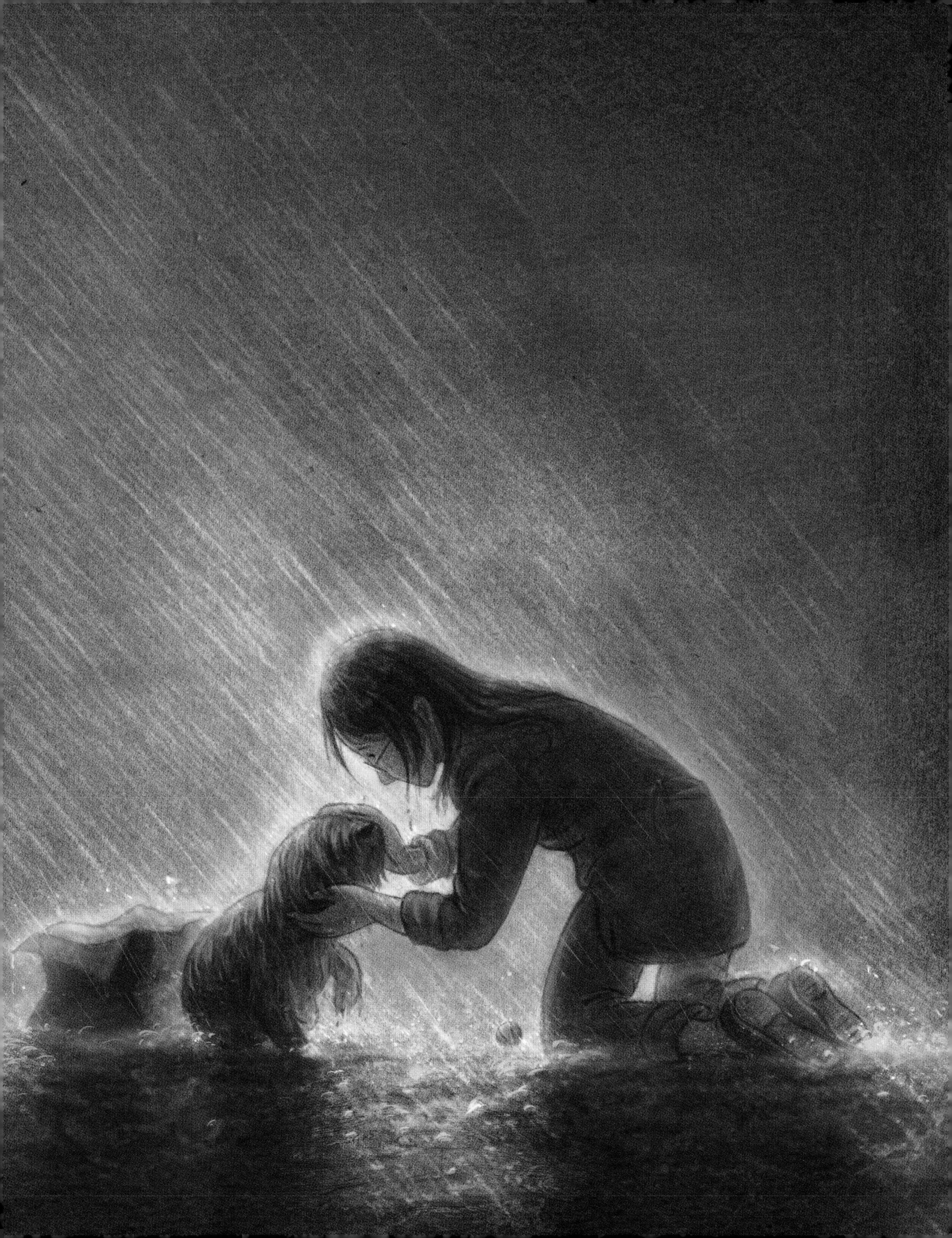

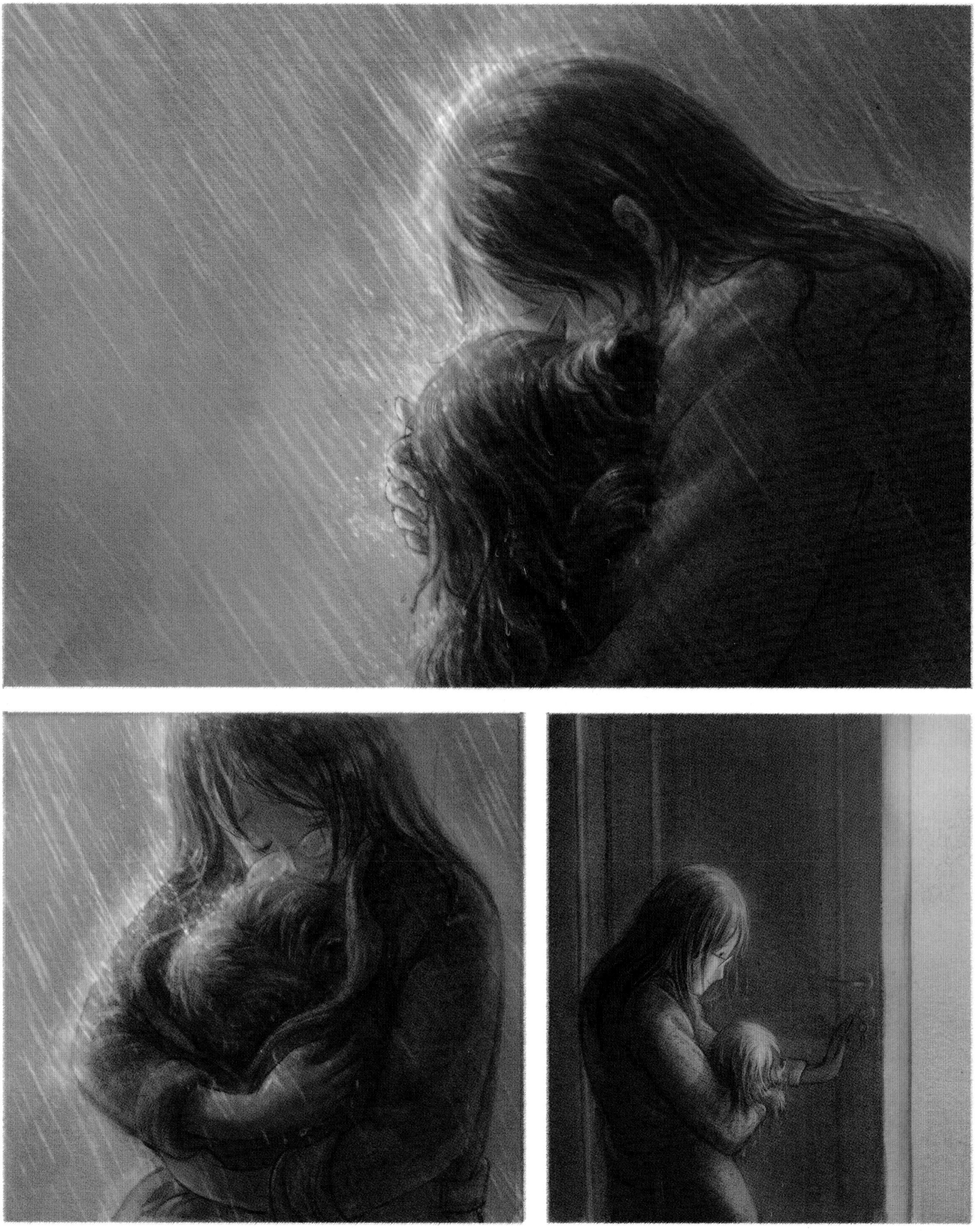

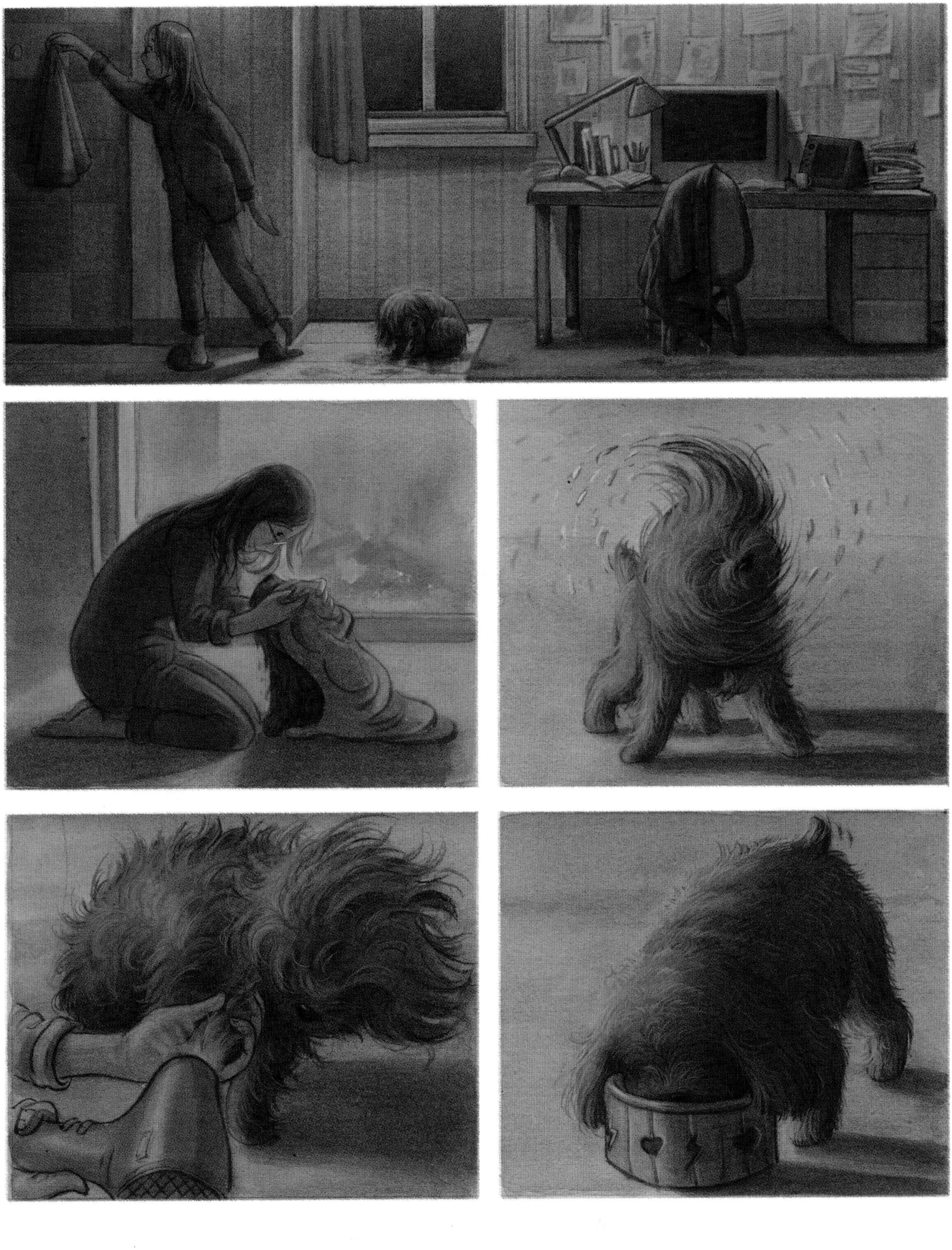

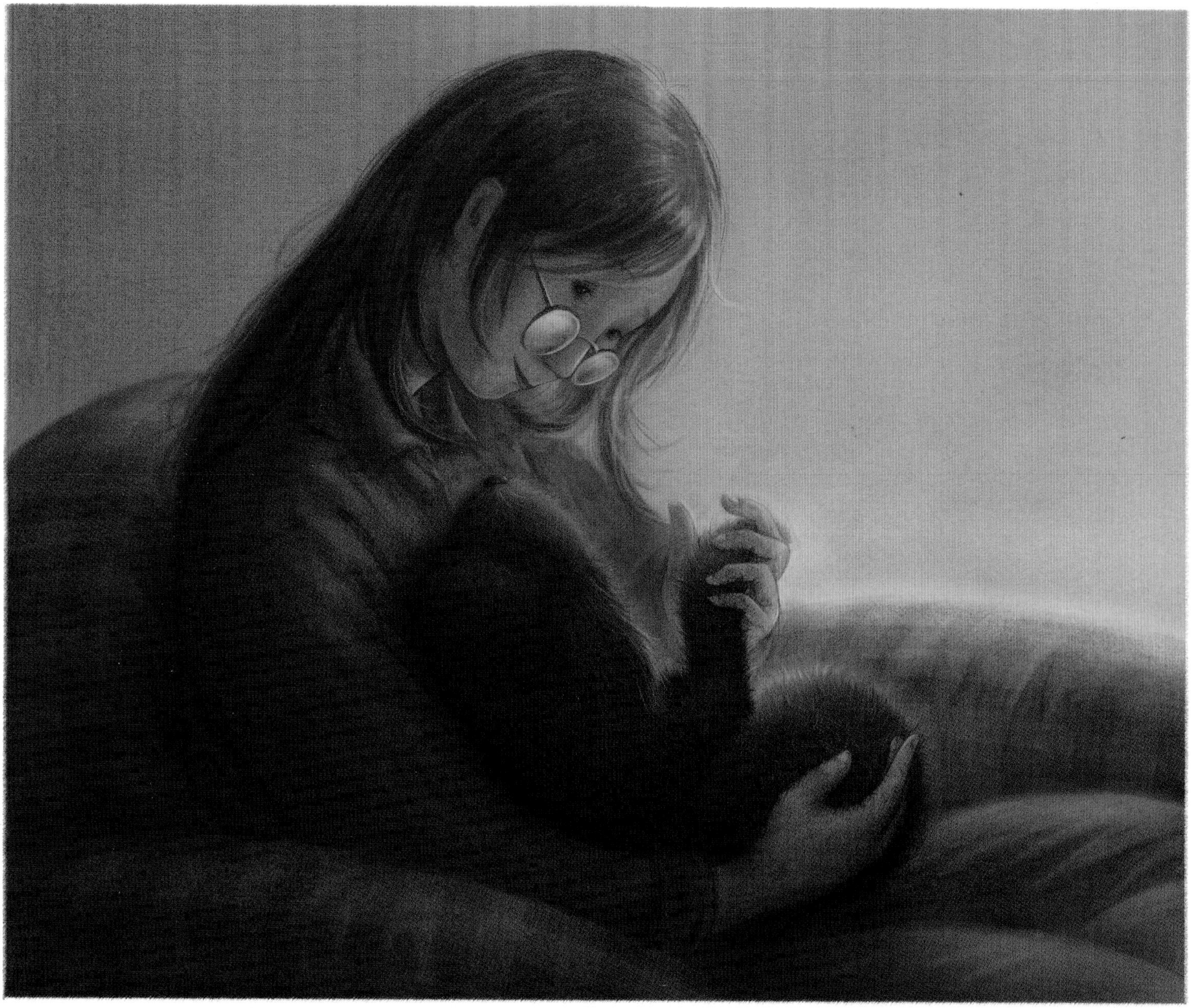

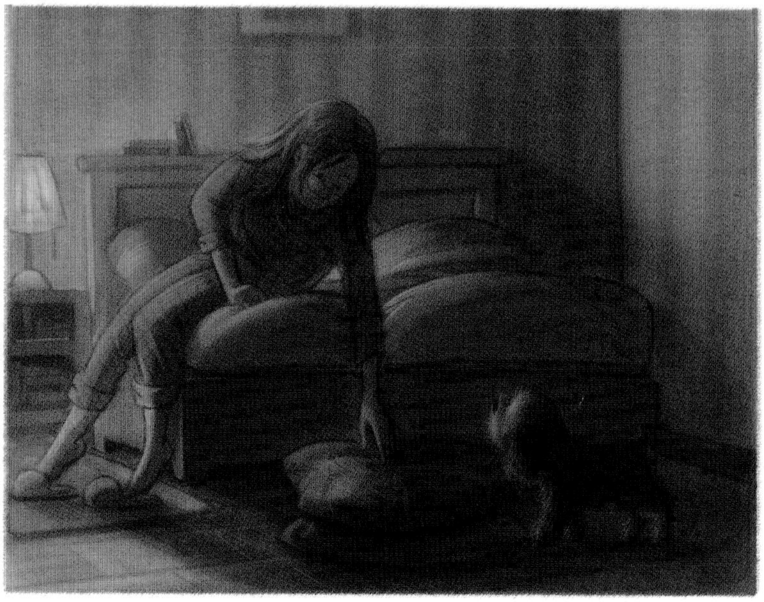

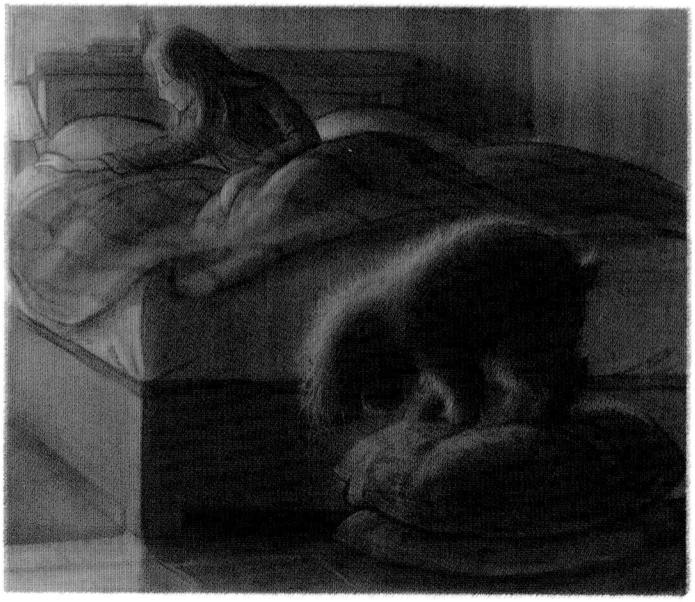

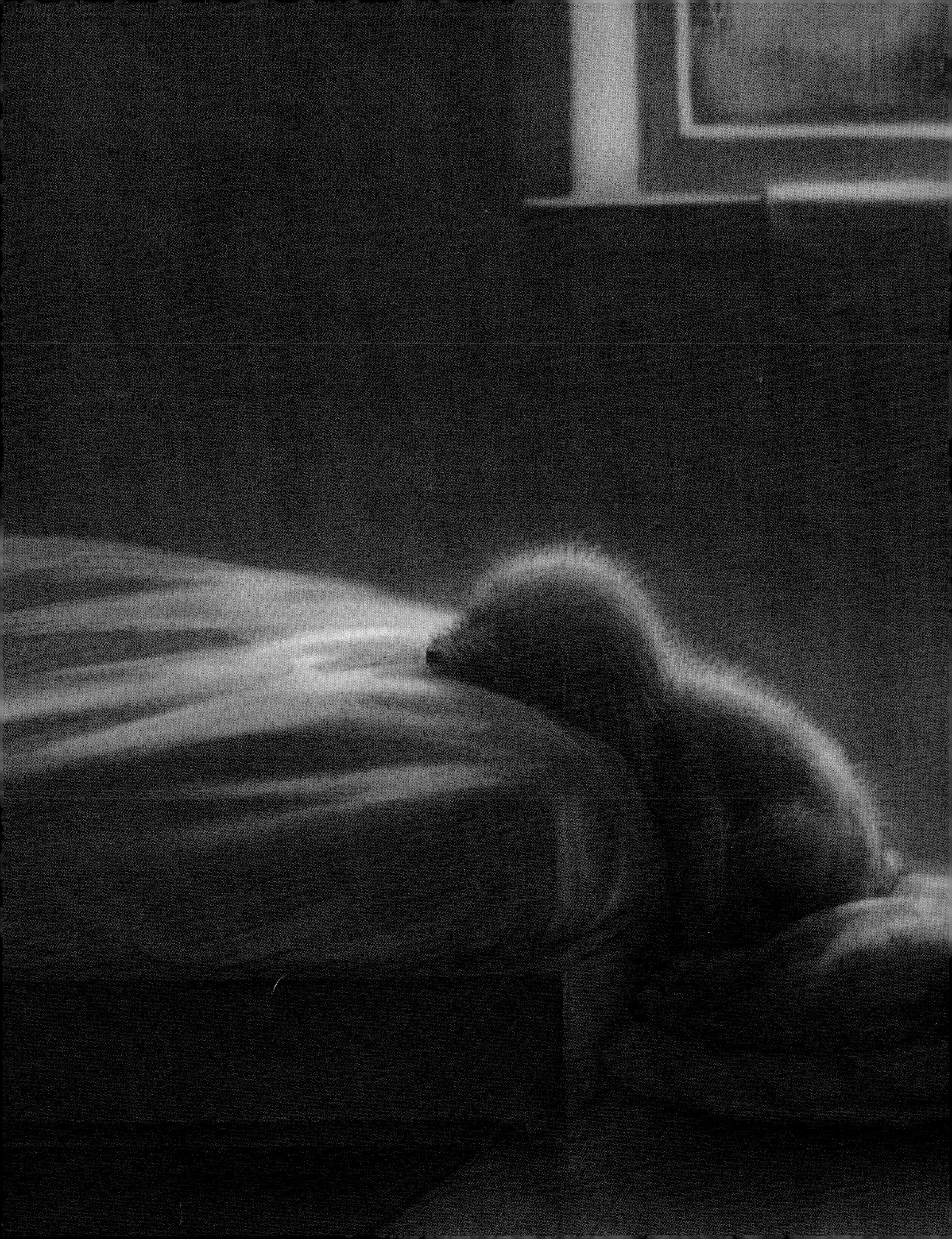

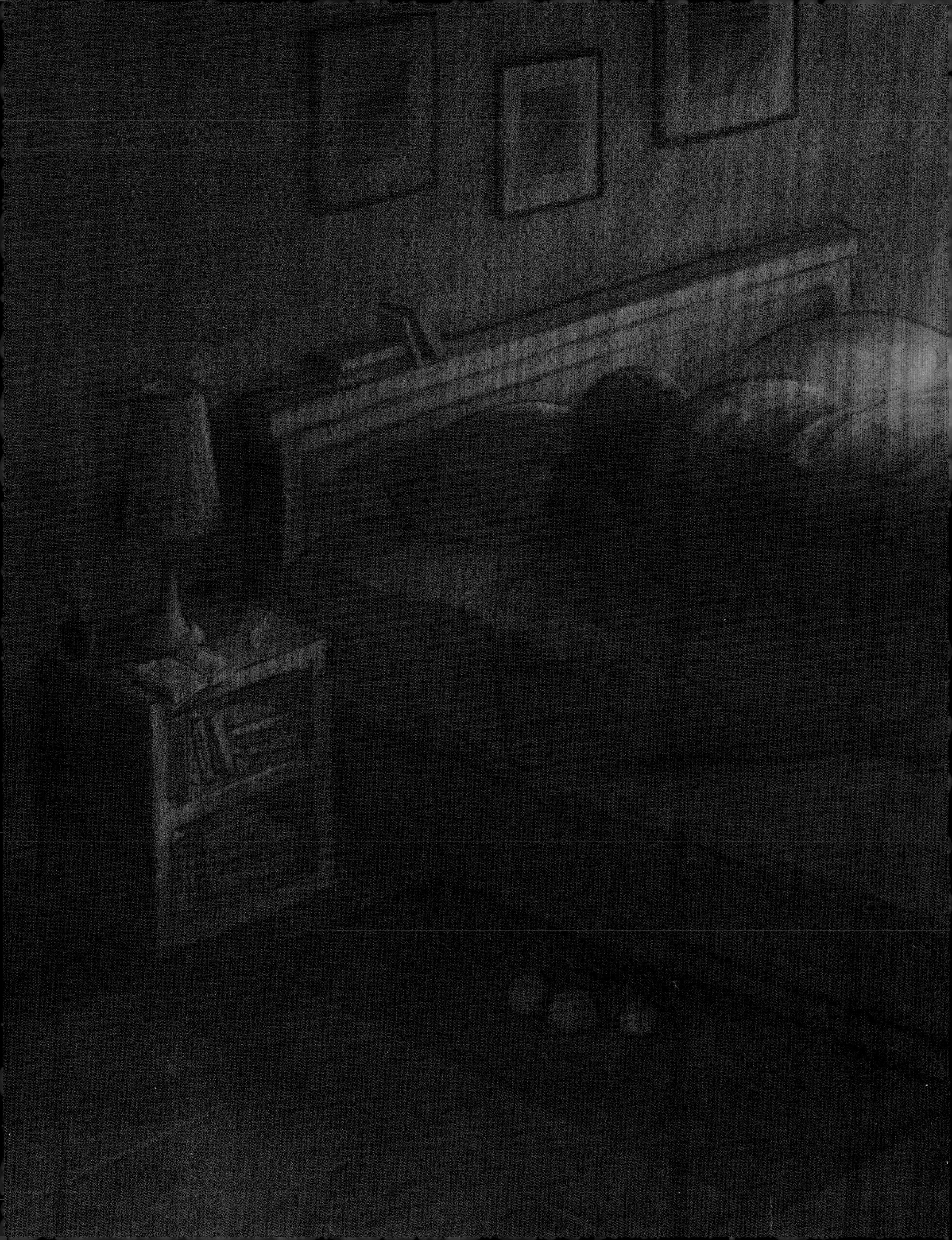

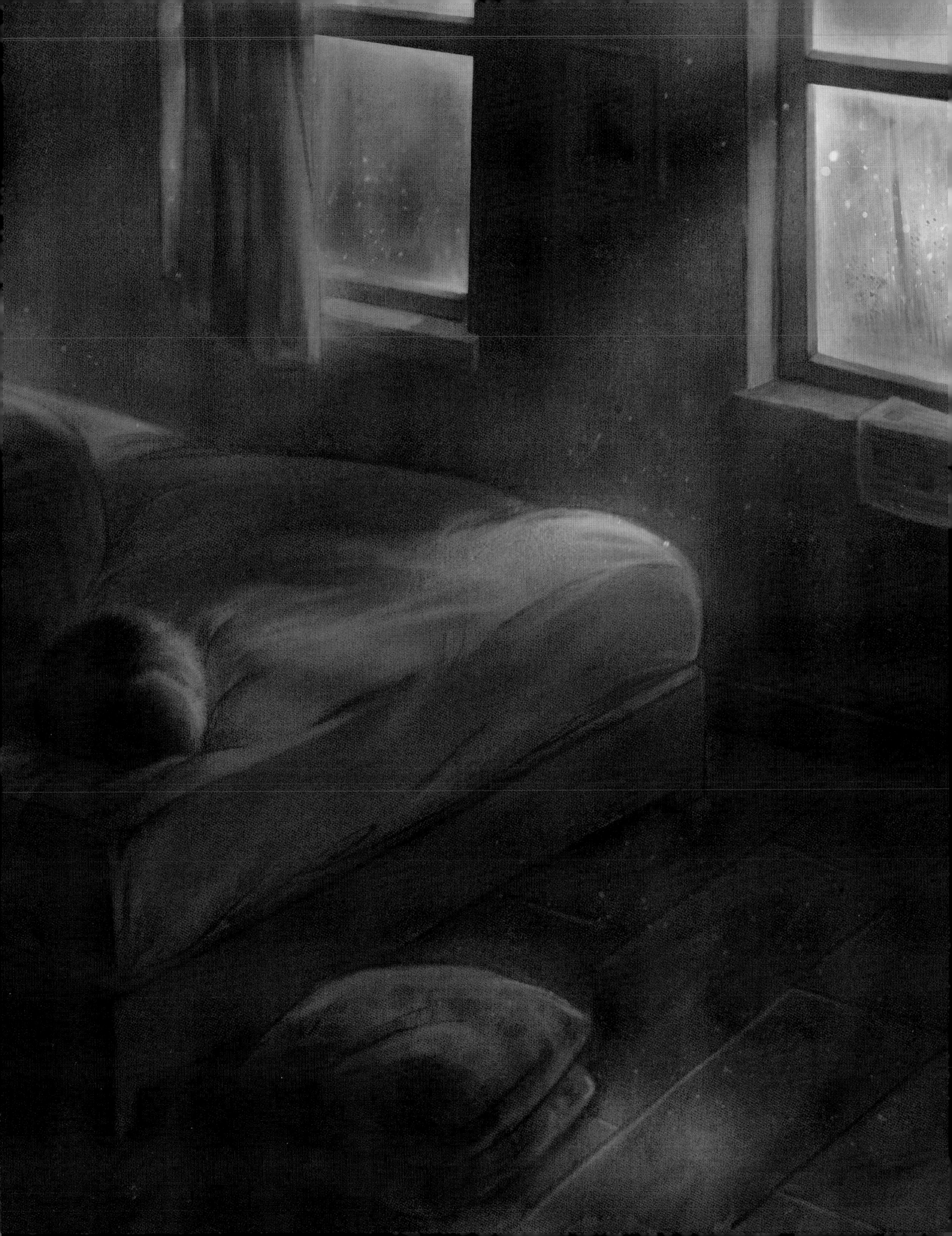

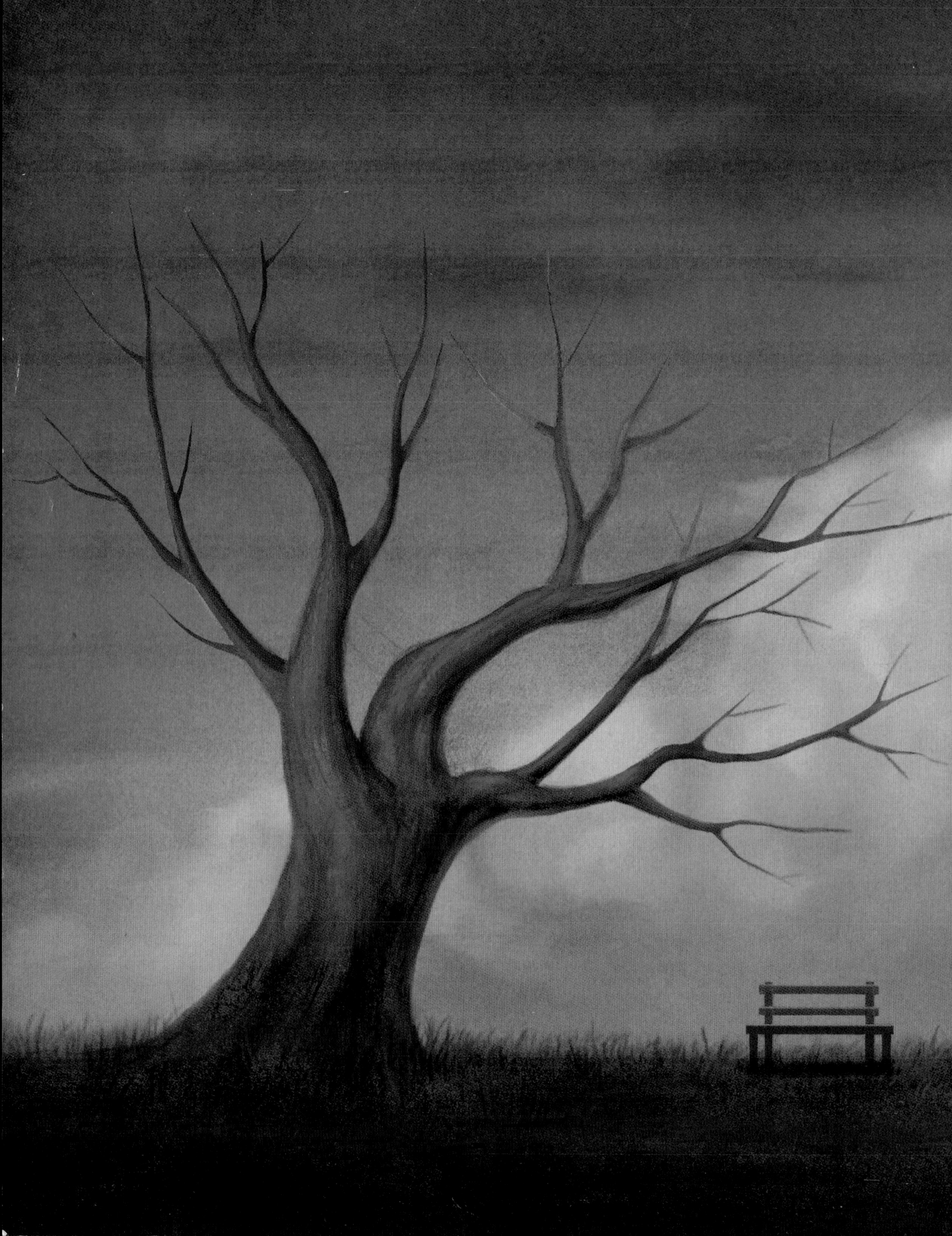